THE SOUND

OF A

RAINBOW

The animals in this book were in no way mistreated and all scenes in which they appear were under strict supervision with the utmost concern for their well-being.

Library and Archives Canada Cataloguing in Publication

Title: The sound of a rainbow / Sharon Frayne.
Names: Frayne, Sharon, 1953- author.
Identifiers: Canadiana (print) 20230145248 | Canadiana (ebook) 20230145272 | ISBN 9781988989594
  (softcover) | ISBN 9781988989600 (EPUB)
Classification: LCC PS8611.R396 S68 2023 | DDC jC813/.6—dc23

Printed and bound in Canada on 100% recycled paper.
Cover Artwork: Monique Legault
Author Photo: Heather Douglas

Published by:
Latitude 46 Publishing
info@latitude46publishing.com
Latitude46publishing.com

We acknowledge the support of the Ontario Arts Council for their generous support.

ONTARIO ARTS COUNCIL
CONSEIL DES ARTS DE L'ONTARIO
an Ontario government agency
un organisme du gouvernement de l'Ontario

THE SOUND

OF A

RAINBOW

SHARON FRAYNE

46

To the kids who feel different, and to their loved ones, who make a difference.

WHY AM I SO MESSED UP?

~~~~~~~~

Suzi Lee, the once-famous pop singer, who was also my mother and professional manager, slapped a brochure on the kitchen table and shoved it at me.

"Raven—are you listening to me? You start tomorrow. And I don't want to hear any arguments."

I looked up from my phone. The brochure she'd passed to me was for a kids' summer camp. Even though it was early August, I shivered. All morning, Suzi'd been on her phone with her office, and hadn't noticed me using a fake account to creep my old stage name. That had become my latest obsession. Months before, I'd deleted all my personal social media accounts, but the cyberbullies and trolls continued their nasty ways. YouTube and TikTok were

1

full of parodies that trashed me.

Suzi also didn't notice that I was still dressed in my pajamas at noon, and hadn't put away the cereal box, or wiped up the spilled strawberry jam and burnt toast crumbs on the counter. Even my own mother didn't care that my life had been destroyed by social media.

"Don't give me that face." She wagged a manicured finger in front of my nose. "This is a great opportunity. We're lucky to get you registered so late this summer. Dr Hill recommended it, and your father and I agreed with her."

"Yeah? Well, I'm not going. I'm almost sixteen. I can do whatever I want."

Suzi put her hands on her hips. There was a little twitch at the corner of her eye. That happened whenever she was stressed. Since *the incident,* stressed would be an understatement. For all of us. She resumed her lecture.

"Raven, it's been over six months. You just stay in the house. You haven't gone to school. Your father and I decided this camp will help you get a fresh start in the fall." For the briefest moment, there was a flicker of softness on her face, then it was back to business. "It's the *only* thing Jon and I have agreed on in years!"

I glanced at the brochure. On the front cover was a close-up photo of a red-nosed clown, wearing a tie-dye shirt and a green bowler hat. In the sky behind him was a picture of a unicorn flying over a rainbow. It looked like something from a cartoon show.

The words written under the photo jumped out at me.

We connect campers to a safe, natural environment, not the internet.

No electronic devices are allowed at camp.

"What?" I read on.

Our trained staff provides caring support for teens in a

remote setting in northern Ontario.

"This is bullshit. You just want to get rid of me." I scrunched the brochure into a ball and flicked it across the table. "Your stupid plans for my career wrecked my life. Nothing's gonna change that. You can't make me go to a friggin' camp!"

Suzi met my eyes, like she wanted to say something, but her phone went off again.

"This is an important call." She turned around and left the room.

I grabbed the balled-up brochure, and ripped it to pieces. Then I put another slice of bread into the toaster. A giant lump filled my throat. I wanted to scream, but all that came out was a pitiful croak. Like I'd swallowed a frog. I pulled up my sleeve and scratched my wrist.

It didn't take long to make the scabs bleed.

THE MIDDLE OF NOWHERE

~~~~~~

We left Toronto early in the morning, before the commuter traffic snarled the highways, and drove north for hours and hours. I kept my eyes closed, and ear buds in. Besides being boring, the drive gave me plenty of time to think about my messed-up life. Occasionally, I checked my phone for outliers from the troll army.

Jon wasn't in the car with us. He'd come by the house to say goodbye. Acting like it was all fine, he'd hugged me and said, "You'll have a wonderful time, sweetheart. This camp could change your life. You'll meet more kids, make some friends, and learn how to swim."

He handed me a package wrapped in silver foil. "Here's a little gift for you to use at camp. When you come back home, you can visit Mia and me in our new place. We'll see you on weekends and holidays. Things will change. Promise!"

His cheerful voice was phony. I'd worked in the entertainment world long enough to recognize someone putting on an act.

"The only change I want is for everything to be like it was," I said. "Before. Before you and Suzi destroyed your marriage. Before you met someone else and left us. Before I worked on that lousy show."

Jon stepped away from me, like I had an infectious disease. "I'm sorry you feel that way, hon. I know you're hurt. No one can undo life's bad stuff. We have to move on and try to make it better. Even when it's hard. I hope someday you'll understand."

He tried to kiss my cheek, but I turned my face away. He left the house and went back to his new girlfriend.

When we were far enough north, in an area where the road went through open tunnels blasted into pink granite, and wound around lakes and trees, my cell coverage died. No more music. I passed the time by daydreaming plans to run away from camp, from my parents, from the bad things that happened. Start over. Where nobody recognized me.

It could work, I thought. *I already look different.*

When I had a singing career, Suzi had me grow my hair long and dye it blond. After I quit, I cut my hair super short and let it go back to my natural colour. Now, it was black and spikey. There were no more hours of styling and makeup. No more public appearances. Just the real me, zits and all.

We stopped for lunch at a roadside place with a big parking lot, a gas bar and WiFi. Inside, I ordered a tuna wrap with no onions, a strawberry yoghurt and a vanilla latte. Suzi ordered a large black coffee, a chicken panini and a Nanaimo bar for us to split.

We sat at a small table for two at the far end of the building, away from the other travelers. Suzi took out her phone and scrolled through her messages.

"You know Dr. Hill said I needed privacy." When I opened the tuna wrap, I smelled the onion and picked it out. I hate onions. "What if the people at the camp recognize me?"

"They won't. When I registered you, I used your middle name as your last name. Since you've gained weight and stopped dying your hair, you look different. No one will know that Raven Lacey used to be Viva Tantie."

My face burned. "Thanks for the reminder." I broke the Nanaimo bar in half and licked off the top layer of chocolate. She went back to her phone and I ate her piece.

At the gas pump, Suzi filled the tank and splashed gasoline on her new dress. She flipped out and ranted about how hard her life was, and how everyone and everything was conspiring against her. It was always someone else's fault.

The gas smell gave me a headache.

For the next hour of the trip, we had cell coverage and she talked to her boss. After I heard Suzi say, "She doesn't want to sing anymore, and we respect that. Her doctor says she could get better, but what happens next is up to her."

I put in my ear buds, shut my eyes and blocked out the rest of the conversation.

Suzi was in charge of recruitment at Top Teen Talent—TripleT for short—a talent show filmed in Toronto. Once a year, twenty teens were selected to compete, and in each episode, one was eliminated. She was on a constant search for fresh talent to audition. After a long tryout process, she'd booked me for the most recent show. In order to avoid problems later on, she asked me to call her and Dad by their first names.

"It sounds more professional," she said.

We drove past Sudbury and continued north on secondary roads. Houses, shopping malls, roadside signs and traffic disappeared. In the middle of a forest, potentially full of wild animals, we pulled into a parking lot on the edge of Pike Lake. We'd reached what Suzi called, 'the Middle of Nowhere.'

On the far side of the lot, beside muddy trucks, men in hard hats and safety vests pointed into the distance and waved their arms. Two guys from a construction crew were erecting a billboard with a picture of condo towers overlooking a beach.

COMING SOON.
LUXURY WATERFRONT CONDO LIVING

A tall man in a business suit stood at the bottom of a large communication tower talking on his phone.

"Progress is everywhere. Even here," Suzi said as she parked beside a dirty truck hooked up to a trailer full of equipment. After putting her phone away, she checked her lipstick, and put on a floppy hat and oversized sunglasses. She stepped out of the car, walked to the back and yanked my suitcase out of the truck.

I stayed inside, locked the door and yelled out the window at her. "You can't force me to stay. As soon as I can, I'm gone."

Suzi held her head high, squared her shoulders and walked off. Her high heels wobbled as she dragged my suitcase through the stones and around the water-filled potholes. Partway across the lot, she turned and yelled at me.

"After *all* I've done for you . . . don't be such a drama queen. It's only three weeks. Camp Rainbow Wings is on an island, so don't even think about leaving."

She left the suitcase and trudged back to the car. When she

leaned in the window, her tone changed.

"Sweetheart, this will be good for you ... it'll be fun. Out in the fresh air, close to nature. Maybe you'll be able to sing again."

That was a low blow. I was going to offer to pull my own suitcase, but when she talked about singing, I lost it. She headed back to the abandoned suitcase. I grabbed my jacket, got out of the car and ran after her.

"An island? Surrounded by water? I can't swim!" I felt sick. "And you know I'll *never* be able to perform again. Not after—"

She stopped, grabbed my hands and looked into my eyes. "Sweetheart, what happened was an accident. I know in my heart, you didn't intend to ..." She couldn't finish the sentence and let my hands go. The silence sat between us, and she looked away.

"Let's put the past behind us and move forward. Isn't that what Dr. Hill suggested?"

A blast from a small ferry boat tied at the wharf interrupted us. We both turned to stare at the boat. The name, *Poseidon, was* painted in gold lettering on the side. The ferry was for foot passengers only, with two decks, a tiny enclosed cabin, and a chimney that belched black smoke.

It was a windy day. The lake looked rough, and waves splashed over the sides of the concrete sidewalk. Gulls squawked and circled overhead and birds ran through the puddles. On the dock near the *Poseidon*, a shifting group of kids and adults stood beside a large folding sign.

"That's where we'll wait." Suzi pointed to the crowd. "When I talked to the camp director, he said the trip to the other side takes thirty minutes." She checked her watch. "It'll be ready to load soon."

I dragged my feet and glanced back at the parking lot where the construction trucks dwarfed Suzi's BMW. I had a horrible sensation that if I stayed, something bad was going to happen.

"I don't belong here. I want to go home."

As usual, Suzi ignored me and plowed on towards the others.

"Fine." I didn't want to make a scene in public, so I followed, then grabbed the suitcase away from her and got ahead.

When I got closer to the boat, I noticed a couple of the kids were in wheelchairs. Near them, was a big guy. Real big. He was so large, he towered over everyone else. Another boy, about my age, had on a hockey jersey and helmet.

There was a younger boy in a blue ball cap, with a red harness buckled over his chest. A leash connected him to a stick-thin woman with long brown hair tied back in a ponytail.

When a gull swooped over his head, he jerked and pulled to the side. The leash almost yanked the woman off her feet. She looked frazzled and tired. The *Poseidon*'s horn blasted a second time, and the boy shrieked and put his hands over his ears. The woman took oversized red headphones out of a bag, and adjusted them over his head.

I was close enough to hear what she said.

"Okay Superman, we have to protect your superpowers. It's time for your special sound-shield." She turned to the other parents.

"I'm sorry. I know this doesn't look good. Loud noise is his kryptonite."

Her words were apologetic but her tone was straightforward. Like she'd had to do this many times before.

"When we land on Rainbow Island, Ash will be fine, and I'll take the harness off. He's got terrible anxiety and this keeps him safe. When he's upset, he tries to run away. The waves terrify him. This boat ride's going to be hard for him. If he panics, he could fall overboard. This trip's way too much stimulation, but it's the only safe way he can get to camp."

9

The other parents nodded, and one mother put a hand on the woman's shoulder.

Leash-boy freaked me out.

I dragged my suitcase farther along the dock to a less crowded spot. Suzi followed me, head down, her face shielded by the hat and sunglasses, as if she was embarrassed to be seen with me. Everyone shrieked and covered their ears when the *Poseidon's* whistle blasted a third time. A tall guy with dreadlocks, wearing shorts, a tie-dye t-shirt and a top hat, stepped off the boat and attached a gangplank bridge from the dock onto the ship's deck.

He seemed confident and friendly, and I assumed he was a camp leader.

Top-hat strolled the length of the deck and yelled, "All aboard for Camp Rainbow Wings! We leave in five minutes!"

Suzi's phone buzzed and she yanked it out of her purse. Her eyes widened, and she took a deep breath before she answered.

The other kids and parents walked along the gangplank onto the ship. Leash-boy shouted something, and started to resist. His mother and Top-hat had to convince him to walk on. The butterflies in my stomach flapped their wings.

She glanced over, blew me a kiss and pointed at the boat.

"Get on, sweetheart. Go without me. I won't get good cell reception on the water, and I have to take this call. We can talk in a few days."

In the background, from the ferry's deck, the boy screamed something that didn't make any sense. Crocodiles? What was he talking about? Everyone else was on board, and Top-hat, waved at us. He yelled, "Don't be slow ... it's time to go! WOW! This ship leaves NOW!"

"SUZI! Please...I don't want to!"

My mother turned her back, and headed towards the car. As

she wandered away, talking on the phone, her voice was loud and bitter. "He won't get away with this. He's the one who cheated. I couldn't care less about that woman and her kid."

I didn't want to hear any more, so I grabbed the handle of my suitcase and ran for the Poseidon.

A STRANGE QUESTION

~~~~~~~~~~~

The *Poseidon* was crowded, and I decided to keep a safe distance from the others. Several of the parents hugged their kids, held their hands or laughed and waved at the people on the shore. Top-hat made terrible rhymes and jokes while we travelled. The others all thought he was hilarious. I thought he was irritating.

The engine hummed, the floor vibrated and rocked, and waves splashed over the side rails of the boat. Out on the lake, the wind was strong and cold, and I buttoned my jean jacket. It was too rough to stand, so I sat alone on a bench and watched the mainland disappear.

Suzi was right about one thing. The trip took thirty minutes. I took out my phone, checked the time and tried to get a signal.

It was weak.

Just holding the phone felt good. I *loved* my phone. The tiny gems on the pink case looked like real diamonds and my stage name, Viva Tantie, was swirled into the pattern. It had been a fifteenth birthday gift from a TripleT sponsor .

The signal disappeared, and the internet was lost. In the distance, I noticed the hazy blue outline of an island, covered by a thick forest.

When we got nearer, I saw a big sign stuck in the tall shore grass.

Welcome to Rainbow Island
and Camp Rainbow Wings.
Where Everyone Can Soar.

A wide, bright rainbow, that stretched over a campground scene, dominated the sign. A tiny, golden-horned unicorn with striped wings flew over the rainbow. The painted face of a red-nosed clown surrounded by smiley red-nosed kids appeared in the background. It was just as cheesy as the brochure. Cheesier.

The horn blasted, Leash-boy shrieked, the other kids cheered and clapped. We bumped against the dock and Top-hat jumped out and secured the *Poseidon* to the dock. Unloading was total chaos. We dragged our suitcases and lugged pillows off the boat, then walked to the shore. Leash-boy's mother removed his headphones and unhooked the harness.

"Follow the yellow-brick road!" Top-hat directed everyone towards the dirt path to the office. "But look out for the frogs and toads."

I wondered if I could turn around, and take the boat back to the mainland. But Suzi would have long since driven away. I didn't have a solid plan. I was stuck.

This is temporary, I told myself.

Using both hands, I hauled my suitcase and followed the other kids and their parents through a sports field surrounded by pine trees. There were paved courts for basketball and tennis. Top-hat pointed to a spot under a tree, and said to wait to be called into the Registration Office.

"It's a lovely day, take a seat if you may. All are welcome here … and your time is coming near."

What could I say? It was so obvious. The campers were different and he was a weirdo. Was that a prerequisite to be at this camp? What did that say about me?

One by one, the other kids and their parents were called inside. I was numb, in a state of shock, but after a while, I got bored and glanced around.

The camp was a large complex, filled with buildings and areas for different activities. Everything was run-down. As if the owners didn't have enough cash or staff for maintenance. The grey paint on the buildings was faded and blistered, and all the flowers in the planters were half-dead.

However, for a place in the middle of nowhere, it was noisy. And hot. After dragging the suitcase, I was sweaty, so I pushed my sleeves up and took a deep breath. Random birds chirped in the trees above me and a little red squirrel, the size of a rat on steroids, came close and stood on its hind legs. It had rings around its eyes and a scrunchy face, like a tiny, angry monkey. When it opened its mouth, I swear it yelled at me.

Get lost, city girl! Go back where you belong.

It was creepy. I gave it the middle finger.

Figures, I thought. *Even the wild animals don't like me.*

A blue ATV covered with dust roared across the sports field

towards the main office. As the quad got closer, the furry red devil sneered, then cursed in squirrel language and ran up the tree.

The ATV slowed and stopped near the building's steps, and the driver shut off the engine. After taking off a helmet and driving gloves, he put on a battered green bowler hat, and adjusted it. Holding onto the frame of the ATV for support, he slowly stepped out. He was ancient, somewhere between sixty and two-hundred, with a big belly and a heavy limp. Messy grey hair came to his shoulders, and his grey beard was frizzy. He was dressed in the same tie-dye camp T-shirt as Top-hat, and wore a beaded necklace.

He walked up the wooden ramp to the office and stopped for breath at the top, wheezing and gasping. I wondered if he was having a heart attack. He leaned against the deck railings, shielded his eyes and squinted into the sunlight. Then he spotted me.

"Who are you and what are you hiding from? Come on up here, child."

Despite calling me *child,* he sounded friendly, so I dragged my suitcase up the ramp and approached him.

"Greetings, Daughter of the Earth. Welcome to Camp Rainbow Wings. You're going to have a blast here."

Right. Who did he think he was? A time traveler from the hippy days?

His voice was rough and gravely, like he had a sore throat. Kinda like mine, but not for the same reason. I figured he was a heavy smoker or drinker, maybe both.

He lifted his hand to give me a high-five. I didn't respond.

Then he grinned; he had a gap where he'd lost some teeth! Yuck. We stood there, kind of awkward, then he tipped his silly green hat and said, "Jelly Bean."

I didn't know how to handle the situation, so I stayed put, with my mouth hanging open. Did he just ask if I wanted some candy? I wasn't a little kid, although I *was* hungry.

"Nice to meet you, Mr.—"

"Jelly Bean. JB, if you prefer. I'm the head clown here. Been here for thirty years now and loved each minute. And you are?"

He held out his hand, and I couldn't help myself. I shook it.

"Raven. I'm not staying."

Maybe it was the croaky sound in my voice, because he held my hand a second longer than expected. His hand felt enormous—swollen and warm. I was embarrassed, but at least right from the start, I'd been honest. When I quit and left, I'd have given him fair warning.

"That's okay, Raven. You can make your own choices here." He squeezed my hand, just a little, but enough that my arm tensed. Like he'd given me a shock from a hand buzzer. An old clown trick.

I jerked, and pulled my hand away. My sleeve was still pushed up, and he saw the marks on my wrist.

Our eyes met, and I pulled down my sleeve.

After a moment of silence, he said the weirdest thing. "Raven, what sound does a rainbow make?"

I figured he was joking. "Honk, honk?"

He laughed, even though my answer wasn't funny.

"I hope we can change your mind. Let's get you started. Head on into the reception area."

He pulled the squeaky screen door open and I stepped through.

LIBERATED?

~~~~~~~~~

Blink. I blinked again, as my eyes tried to adjust to the dim light inside. The air smelled musty. I used to worry that stuff like that would damage my voice. Now, not so much. The office was crammed full of junk, but nobody else was there. I found a old chair that faced a large aerial photograph, and sat down. *Creak!* While I waited, I studied the photo.

Interesting. When I squinted, the details came into focus. The photo showed a bird's eye view of the Pike Lake area, including the mainland, lake, Rainbow Island, and a group of nearby small islands. The Rainbow Wings campground occupied half of the island. The rest was a wilderness. A medium sized island, that didn't look too far away from the camp, was labelled *Treasure Island*.

The office desk was piled with computer equipment, clipboards and containers of pens and markers. A large glass jar full of mixed candies sat on the desk corner. At the back of the office was another room with a sign on the door: *Infirmary*.

I heard adult voices coming from inside the Infirmary, discussing someone's medication requirements. So much for privacy.

The entire place resembled a worn out set from an old-time movie. The furniture was battered and tacky. Thankfully, no one had hung horrible, glassy-eyed stuffed animal heads on the walls. And there were no toilet seat lids mounted with antler racks from dead deer.

Clustered on a side wall were photos of the camp taken throughout the years. In them, lots of kids were dressed like clowns with red-noses, but there were also photos of kids in different costumes, and scenes of camp activities.

It seemed more than clowning happened at Rainbow Wings.

I got up and grabbed a camp brochure from the desk, and shoved it in my pocket. There were loads more pictures to look at. Old black-and-white images in black plastic frames. Photos of a band. Rock concerts. No one was there to watch me, so I moved in for a closer look.

Most of the band photos were of the same five guys. Three guitars, a keyboard player, and a wild-looking drummer. It was Jelly Bean! Taken when he was a lot younger, and cute in a hairy, goofy way. One photo, taken from the stage, showed an enormous crowd at an outdoor concert. There was a close up of him pounding his drum kit's cymbal. In all the pictures, he had the same gap-toothed grin.

In another picture, set outside a hospital tent, the younger version of Jelly Bean kissed a pretty medic. I stared at the details in the photos. Many of the scenes looked vaguely familiar.

When an older woman in a tie-dye camp t-shirt walked out from the Infirmary, I backed away and sat down on the squeaky chair again.

I blinked again. This time, because I was startled. She was the medic from the photo, but heavier, with long grey hair. She'd aged, but it was definitely her.

She sat behind the desk, put on her glasses and shuffled some papers.

To get her attention, I coughed, and tugged my suitcase closer. The wheels squealed on the wood floor. She jumped at the noise.

"Oh, I'm so sorry! You must be Raven! Welcome to camp, dear. I wasn't trying to ignore you, just a bit distracted at the moment." She took off her glasses, and the lines around her eyes crinkled when she smiled.

"I'm Kirra Pike, the camp doctor. Your mother called and said she was sorry she wasn't able to come. But she's sent me all your information."

She paused and looked thoughtful. "Is there anything else you'd like to add?"

Before I could tell her I already hated the camp and planned to leave on the next ferry, we were interrupted.

Top-hat, the counselor from the ferry, came out of the Infirmary with Leash-boy and his mom. The boy had a mop of red hair and looked about eleven or twelve. She'd removed his harness, but his walk was stiff, and his whole body jerked as he looked around the room.

His mom's voice was soft, almost a whisper, but I overheard bits and pieces.

"—difficult personality disorder . . . not sure . . . doctors say it's complex neuro-divergence... struggled . . . used to talk . . . trauma . . . hardly says a word—"

19

Top-hat nodded. "Okay. That's helpful information."

As she handed Top-hat the harness, the mother's hand trembled, but her words were clear. "We call this his 'Superman Safety-strap.' It keeps him safe if he panics and tries to run. It's especially important in noisy places or near water. At least until he settles. Ash is quite intelligent ... but after his father. . . he—"

Her voice broke and she wiped her eyes. "Sorry."

After a deep breath she continued. "My fiancé says camp will help. Ash needs one-on-one support at all times. In September, he's registered in an intensive therapy placement. It has a great reputation."

She choked and struggled for self-control. "My son has lots of potential. He was smart and athletic. I don't believe it's all gone. We like that this is an inclusive camp, so Ash will be with neuro-typical teens. We hope that Camp Rainbow Wings will help him develop confidence and independence."

While she talked about him, Leash-boy continued to glance around the room, checking out the decorations and furniture. When he saw me sitting on the chair, he froze. Then, in a yell as loud as a balloon bursting, he yelled, "HA!"

He took a step closer and flung out his arm. His hand knocked over the glass jar on the edge of Kirra's desk, and the candy spilled on the floor.

"Oh, Ash! You have to be careful." His mother's face turned red.

"Five second rule," I said, and knelt to collect the peppermints that had rolled towards me. Ash sat down cross-legged and gathered the sour balls and jawbreakers that had gone under Kirra's desk. Not knowing where else to put them, I dropped the candies back into the jar.

He had other ideas.

He took a handful, juggled them in the air, and caught one in his mouth.

Incredible. I burst into laughter and gave a thumbs up.

"Hey, Superman ... that's awesome! Watch me!" I flipped a pink mint in the air and tried to catch it with my mouth. It landed on my nose and bounced onto the floor. "Oops!"

He clapped his hands, laughed and said, "HA!"

Top-hat laughed, then everyone laughed and started to toss candy. For a brief moment, there was a shower of mints and caramels. Of course, no one else caught them.

Leash-boy's mother patted his shoulder and turned to me. "Thank you, that was very kind. You did the right thing. Will you keep an eye out for Ash? Be his friend at camp?"

Why did she say that?

I stopped laughing and sat back on the chair.

"Ahh ..." I wasn't about to assume any responsibility. It wasn't *my* job. But she looked worried and hopeful; I didn't want to hurt her feelings.

"My dad's a teacher," I said. "Sometimes, when his class went on field trips I helped with the kids who needed extra support." My throat felt swollen, like a lump of clay was stuck half-way. Maybe that's why the words came out lame.

Kirra interjected, "This is Raven Lacey. It's her first time at this camp, too."

Leash-boy's mom's face lit up. "Raven..." She came close and beamed at me. "That's wonderful. I know you'll get along with Ash. He likes you already."

I leaned back, and ended the conversation by pulling out the camp brochure and pretending to study it.

Ash and his mom hugged. She held him for a long moment, then kissed him on the cheek. "Have fun, Superman. I'll see you in a few weeks, and will think about you all the time. Be good and do what they say."

"HA!" Ash flicked his fingers, and his mother gathered her belongings.

Top-hat said, "I'll show you around. You'll be happy you've found ... this wonderful place to give you some space. Your mama's leavin' now, but don't have a cow. Say a quick goodbye, then let your wings fly."

Kirra burst into laughter. "Moe, there's nobody in the world quite like you. Go on ... get out of here, and let me finish Raven's paperwork."

Before they went out the door, Ash's mom said, "Raven, it was so nice to meet you."

Kirra studied her computer screen for a moment after they left, then gasped. "Oh no!" She grabbed some papers and jumped to her feet. "I forgot to get these signed. Wait here, I'll be right back."

Then she ran out the door.

A few older kids dressed in camp t-shirts wandered through the office after this interaction. A handsome guy, tall with short black hair, wearing a camp t-shirt that said *SENIOR COUNSELOR* on the back, walked by. He stopped and turned around.

"Well, hellooooo there ..."

His voice was deep and mellow, and when he grinned at me, I felt light-headed. He was about twenty and had a tattoo of a basketball on his forearm. I couldn't take my eyes off him. When he offered to take me to my cabin, and then show me around the camp, I said, "Sure!" and grinned like an idiot.

As we were about to leave, Kirra came back, still flustered, and said, "Grif, could you please wait outside for your camper? We need a few more minutes to finish some paperwork."

Grif winked and reached for the doorknob. When he opened

the door, a dazzling flash of sunlight flooded into the room. He stepped out, closed the door behind him, and left me blinking in the dimness.

Kirra shuffled through papers and checked things off a list. I yawned and felt cranky and hungry. My stomach growled, and I considered asking for some of the candy we'd picked up off the floor.

I wondered what activities Grif supervised so I opened the brochure and studied what the camp offered. There was a lot to choose from. More than I expected.

Kirra tapped the computer keyboard, then glanced at me. "Sorry, Raven, I've been distracted this morning. Let's start over. I want to give you a proper welcome to Camp Rainbow Wings. You'll love it here. You'll learn to spread your wings and fly."

Maybe it was because I'd had a hard time with Suzi, maybe because I was tired, or maybe because sometimes I'm a brat.

"That's just a stupid marketing slogan," I said. "I don't intend to stay here, or be a clown."

It was mean, but I meant it.

She sighed, took off her glasses and studied me. When she spoke, her voice held a gentle reproach that caught me off guard.

"Raven, let's clear up that misunderstanding. Among other things, JB used to be a professional clown. He still loves to dress up. It's an important part of who he is. But here, we don't clown around."

She crossed her arms and leaned forward. "We have all kinds of campers – including teens with significant challenges in their lives. They're integrated into all aspects of camp. We focus on the performing arts. In our sessions, there's some clowning work, but during the final weeks of camp we rehearse a musical. Everyone participates."

That caught my attention. It was the first I'd heard about

performing arts. I wasn't sure what she meant, or whether I cared. As long as they didn't force me to act like a clown. Being laughed at by the whole world already was enough.

"For this final camp session this summer, we've planned a great show. It's called 'SHIVERS!'. That's short for 'Shiver Me Timbers'. JB will explain it at the first campfire program tomorrow night."

Kirra ignored my sulks, and studied her computer screen. "You're going to have a birthday while you're here. Sixteen! That'll be fun!"

"I doubt it." I mumbled, but she heard me, because her smile disappeared. She handed over more flyers and a schedule and told me to review them in my cabin. Then she said the words I'd dreaded ever since I learned about camp.

"I'm sure you know this is a tech-free environment. Your mother signed the paperwork and sent it through. I need you to hand over your phone, and any electronic devices you've brought. We'll keep them safe at the office, and return them when you leave. Once a week, you'll have an opportunity to connect with your family. If there's an emergency, we can contact them."

I didn't move. My mouth went dry, and I coughed. Tears filled my eyes, just like I'd learned to do as a performer, when I wanted my way. I blinked, letting them trickle over my cheeks.

Kirra held her hand out. "Please."

Reluctantly, I handed over my beautiful phone. I'd had it forever. Almost a year. It felt like she'd robbed me. Like she'd stolen my identity. She smiled like it didn't matter.

But it did!

Kirra leaned over and fumbled under the desk. There was a thud and a click. "Now you're liberated! Your phone is locked in our safe with the others. One more thing—"

She stood and beckoned me to follow her into the infirmary,

then pointed to a stool and asked me to sit. "I need to did a nit check," she said.

Nits! *How much worse could the place get?*

Like all the other medical rooms I'd been in during the past six months, it smelled like cleaning supplies. Staff photos, framed diplomas, and certificates lined the walls. Apparently, a lot of qualified people worked at camp.

"This will take a minute. Everyone has to do it. You don't want to get lice in this beautiful black hair, do you?" Two long wooden sticks were in her hands.

I cringed as she put on gloves, then shuddered and closed my eyes when she pulled the sticks through my hair. It felt feathery and airy, not scratchy as I'd imagined. She didn't take long inspecting my scalp.

"Done! No nits! Your counselor's waiting outside to help you settle in."

As we left the infirmary, the main door opened and the big guy from the ferry and his mother stepped inside the reception room.

I grabbed my stuff and headed outside.

GRIF

~~~~~~~~~~~~~~

I pulled my suitcase through the office door and rolled it down the ramp. Grif was waiting on the bench in the shade, chewing a piece of grass.

"That took a long time. I'll bet you got the stupid lecture and handed over your phone." He winked and his blue eyes sparkled. The way he said it made me smile, even though I was mad about it.

"Yep. What a dumb rule. I don't know if I can survive without it." I dropped the handle of my suitcase, and he shook my hand. His grip was strong and warm, and my knees wobbled.

"Kirra told you my name—Grif. I'm the new senior counselor in charge of waterfront and athletics. I'll walk you to your cabin.

When you're unpacked, I'll take you on a grand tour of Camp Rainbow Wings."

He made a funny face and flapped his arms and I burst out laughing.

"You must be a celebrity or something!" he said. "You're with the first group. Most of the campers arrive tomorrow. What's your name and where are you from?"

"Raven. I'm from Toronto." I didn't want to give him much information, even though being close to him made me dizzy. Even though I was never *actually* famous—just hoped I'd be—I wanted to stay on the safe side. Not that he'd recognize me after I'd changed my hair and wasn't wearing makeup. I wasn't *Viva Tantie,* wannabe star from TripleT, anymore.

He took my paperwork and studied it. "You're in the Bobcat cabin. Follow me!"

Grif walked me to a small log building with a red roof in the middle of a group of identical cabins. The names of animals or birds painted on wooden signs nailed above the doors was the single visible difference. Moose, Deer, Squirrel, Lynx and finally, Bobcat at the end of the row. The cabins had ramps that led to a raised deck and screened-in porch. He pulled my suitcase along the ramp, and parked it by the porch. He leaned against the railing, grinned and put a light hand on my shoulder.

"It's been a long day. You're probably tired. Unpack and settle in. I'll come back in half an hour, tour you around, and go through the schedule. You can choose your activities and sign up for them tomorrow."

Inside the cabin, it was dark and cool, with the same musty odor as the office. I took a moment to get oriented and check it out. There was a big main room with six bunk beds, three on each side of the room, some side tables and a few shelves. In the middle of the room was a table with wooden chairs; storage cupboards lined the walls. At the back, a couple of doors led to private rooms. One was for the counselor who stayed with us at night, I figured, and the other was a bathroom.

Instant relief! I was worried that we'd have to use a stinky outhouse. The oversized bathroom was modified with an open shower, grab bars on the walls and an adapted toilet. It wasn't anything like I was used to, but I didn't care; I didn't plan to stay long.

I chose a bunk at the back, and unpacked my suitcase into the cupboard nearest my bed. At the bottom of my case was the package from my dad. I ripped off the paper and pulled out a journal and a set of pens and markers.

Jon must have remembered that my therapist, Dr. Hill, had suggested I jot things down whenever I was upset. Today seemed like a good day to get started.

On the first page I wrote, *Camp sucks. I need my phone. I want to go home.*

KEEP OUT

~~~~~~~~~~

It didn't take long to finish putting my gear away, and while I waited for Grif, I thought about what had happened to me in the last six months. The bad memories flooded back like they often did. There was a knock at the cabin door, and I grabbed a tissue to wipe my eyes, hoping Grif wouldn't notice.

Grif opened the door and poked his head inside.

"Hey! Raven ... you ready? We'll grab a bite to eat, and I'll show you around."

I took a deep breath, and went out the door.

Grif took me to a big log building with long tables, benches and stacking chairs. The menu was posted on a chalkboard, and food was served cafeteria style. There was a variety of salads and burgers. A choice of beef or veggie. Juice, milk or water. Fresh fruit.

I would have killed for chocolate and a doughnut.

The other kids who came on the boat with me were already sitting at the tables. Each one had a counselor beside them. Apparently, they'd arrived at camp before the others because they needed extra support.

What did that say about me?

After we ate, Grif toured me around.

"When everyone's here, there'll be sixty-five kids, plus their counselors and the adults who live here. The cabins are all accessible."

He walked to the sports fields, and at the basketball court, he shot a few hoops. Next, we visited the campfire pit and seating, and the outdoor stage. Afterwards, we sat together on a bench near the forest.

"That was my first official tour. How'd I do?"

"Great!"

I pointed at a painted yellow sign on a nearby tree that said, **Keep Out. Private Property.** "What's over there?"

He rolled his eyes and waved at the signs posted on all the trees that separated the camp property from the woods.

No Trespassing
Do Not Enter This Area.

"That part of the island used to be a wildlife rehabilitation sanctuary. Now, a demented old lady lives out there. Alone. The whole place is a dump. No one's allowed to go in there. She's got cages."

My stomach twisted. I was already nervous about being surrounded by forest. It was so different from where I lived. What if there were bears hiding in the nearby bushes?

"Doesn't JB own all of Rainbow Island?"

"The camp's a separate property that JB manages. Both places are huge." He yawned, then stared at me, puzzled. "You look familiar. Have we met before?"

Crap. He's on to me. I'd told Suzi this might happen.

I turned away, and said he must be thinking of someone else.

Grif didn't seem like someone who would watch the finals of the TripleT show, and would know about my disastrous performance. Even if he tried to check me out, he wouldn't connect the former Viva Tantie with the new me – Raven Lacey.

Besides—how would he know my true identity if no one was allowed to have a phone?

Then he took out a phone and said he wanted to take my picture!

"I'm the official camp photographer. On the last day, I'll show the video to the camp. It'll be a surprise—especially for JB and Kirra. Don't tell anyone. They might spill the beans."

He laughed at his own joke. "Beans. Jelly. Get it?"

He glanced around to check if anyone was watching, then told me to stand by one of the signs. He had me take a pose with my hands on my hips, head tipped to the side. I ran my fingers through my hair to fluff it, and his expression brightened.

"Wow! That'll be a beautiful photo." He put the phone into a pocket. "Promise now, it's a secret."

Somehow, it didn't feel right. But he'd been so nice to me. It had been a long time since I'd had my picture taken, and having a secret made it feel like I was special.

"I promise."

Grif reviewed the camp map and schedule with me, and reminded me he was the athletic supervisor.

"I work at the waterfront," he said. "Do you like swimming?"

"Love it."

"Great! I'm there in the afternoon. Come in your free time, and we can hang out."

A bell rang outside the café. He said it was the signal to go to the cabins, and walked me along the asphalt path. When we got to Bobcat cabin, an older girl in a wheelchair waited outside.

She didn't look happy.

Her frown froze us in place. She had on the camp t-shirt, and a thick necklace of beads. Long pieces of frizzy brown hair dangled from her messy bun, and her face was red and sweaty. Instead of sounding welcoming, she scolded me like I was a little kid.

"Raven Lacey? I'm Tasha. Your cabin counselor. Where've you been? I was supposed to meet you this afternoon and help you get orientated."

Grif rubbed his hands in his hair. "Sorry, Tasha. I messed up. When she came out of Registration, I thought I was supposed to show her around."

"Okay. These things happen. I got your guy straightened out, Grif, and he's waiting for you at the Bear cabin. Sorry, Raven, I was just worried about you. Let's go inside and get acquainted. Welcome to Rainbow Wings."

ZOMBIES AND PRISON GUARDS

~~~~~~~

In the middle of the first night, a nightmare. I was at a concert, singing in my underwear, and the crowd was laughing. When I woke, I didn't know where I was.

But I was shaking and screamed for help.

I sat up, tried to see, but it was dark. Something moved outside my window. It snorted, and I froze.

Then, it got worse. In the distance, something howled, and something else howled back.

On and on it went. It was a spooky sound, almost like laughing. The hair on my arms prickled. The wails continued, and it seemed to get closer.

It was like werewolves were calling to each other. Or Zombies.

Tasha was asleep in the private room at the back of Bobcat cabin, so I wasn't TOTALLY alone. But it felt like it.

My screams woke her, and she was pissed.

"I'm coming. Give me a minute," she yelled.

When I heard her huffing and thumping around in her bedroom, I felt a little guilty.

It took a while for her to get organized. After a few minutes, she came out of her bedroom and parked the wheelchair beside my bunk.

"What's wrong?"

"Something's outside my window! I think it's a bear." Then we both heard the wails. I grabbed her arm.

"What is that? It's the most horrible sound I've ever heard. Like it's calling from the dead."

"You're not used to the northern woods. I forgot you've always lived in the city."

There was a tone in her voice that I wasn't used to. Was it anger? Scorn?

No. Not at all.

"There's no Zombies here. No raving killer maniacs. Maybe there was a deer outside your window, or a chipmunk. That sound's a pair of loons on the lake, calling to each other. If you've never heard it before, it's strange. But when you get used to it, it's beautiful."

I was embarrassed, and didn't know what to say.

"I'm sorry. I was having a nightmare. Then I heard weird noises. Guess I over-reacted. This is all new to me. Can you stay here for a minute?"

"Sure."

Moonlight coming through the window backlit Tasha's silhouette, outlining her round face and loose hair. Without turning on a light, she poured me a glass of water and sat beside my bed.

We stayed like that for a while, talking in the dark.

Somehow, it was easier than talking in daylight.

After a while, I asked Tasha why she needed a wheelchair. She said that when she was twelve, she was in a car accident. Her dad was driving. Late one night, they were hit head on by a drunk driver. Her dad broke his leg. She was hospitalized for months and then did rehab. She's never going to walk again.

She told me about her first time at camp. "It was a year after the accident and I was terrified, just like you. Believe me, it will get better."

We chatted for a while about camp life, then she said, "Listen, we've got a big day tomorrow. It's time to go back to sleep."

How could I sleep? Between scratching a mosquito bite, flailing at another one buzzing around my head, listening to the howls outside, and worrying about how I'd cope at camp, I was awake the rest of the night.

And—I felt guilty. How could I have known to wait for her after registration? Besides, Grif was new and he just made a simple mistake trying to be helpful.

So it *wasn't* my fault.

As the hours passed, I tried to figure out a plan. There had to be a way to get off the island.

According to what I remembered of the camp schedule, breakfast was at 8:00 A.M. Before she'd gone back to her room, Tasha had said that the other campers would arrive on the ferry in small groups all day. She wanted to meet the LITs—Leaders in Training—assigned to our cabin when they registered.

They were considered the junior counsellors. I'd be only person in our cabin not in that group. I'd have free time to explore, or just hang out while they got organized. As long as I joined them for meals, didn't leave the camp property or go near the waterfront.

Tasha's plan was for the two of us to have breakfast together, and she'd help me choose my activities. Then I'd be on my own until everyone was settled.

With all that going through my head, I couldn't relax. I turned on the light and read over the camp brochure for the hundredth time.

At the bottom of the last page, it said:

**Stay on camp property at all times. DO NOT enter the Private Property area.
**Never go to the waterfront without supervision.
**Stay in your cabin at night after lights out.
**If there's a problem you can't solve on your own, get help from your counselor.
**Be kind. Be honest. Be yourself.

Rules, rules, rules.

Even though I wanted to, I couldn't text Suzi or Jon to take me home because Kirra Pike, the camp doctor/ a.k.a. prison guard, had my phone.

I'd have to figure out another way.

A LIE

~~~~~~~~~~

At breakfast, the air in the cafeteria was hot and sticky, and smelled like pancakes and maple syrup. Behind the serving counter, a tall man with a pointy, waxed moustache and a chef's hat dumped scrambled eggs into a metal dish. Lots of food choices available. All healthy. No pop or doughnuts.

My stomach growled. I scanned the room for Grif, but he wasn't there.

The other kids who'd arrived on the ferry with me sat at a picnic table with their counselors. There was no more room at their table. They already looked like a group of old friends. Ash was off leash and had a massive pile of pancakes on his plate. His chin was covered with brown syrup.

He burped, patted his stomach and in a loud voice, said, "AHHHH!"

Revolting.

Amazingly, no one laughed or told him off. Moe, aka Top-Hat, sat beside him and waved when he saw us.

"Come on over, if you're willing and able. We can make room at this happy table."

Tasha shook her head. "I need more space." I was the only one to hear her mutter, "It's too early for all that energy. Let's go to the other side and we can talk in private."

We took our breakfast trays to a far corner, and I moved some chairs to make room for Tasha. After she'd slathered her pancakes with butter and poured a flood of maple syrup overtop, Tasha was in a chatty mood. Between mouthfuls, she asked about my hobbies and interests.

Obviously, she didn't recognize me, and between spoonfuls of peach yoghurt and blueberries, I invented an alternative life. "I'm the youngest of six kids. I'm here because I won a special scholarship. A service club picked me. My marks were the highest in my class, *and* I was President of the Student Council." That was all a total lie, but it would be easy to remember.

She asked what activities I wanted to sign up for.

"I'm on the school Swim Team and I want to practice here."

"That's great. You'll love camp! Most of the time, we focus on the performance arts. Most of the activities lead to the final show that JB and Moe organize for the parents. Pick your favourites from the list in the brochure. In the free time, you can go swimming. You've already met our new Waterfront Director—the amazing Grif."

Was there sarcasm in her voice?

I pretended to be surprised. "Awesome! I love to swim and

hang out at the beach. He was so nice when he showed me around yesterday."

Tasha gulped a mouthful of orange juice and cut into a link of golden-brown sausage. "I'm sorry I got upset about it. Grif's just started to work here, so he didn't realize it was my job as your cabin counselor. I guess the intention was good. No harm done."

She wiped bits of orange pulp off her mouth and continued.

"The senior staff meets on a regular basis with JB to discuss big-picture camp stuff. My meeting yesterday went overtime, so it was partially my fault. We talked about financial stuff." She winced and took another sip. "I was with Grif's camper all afternoon. Poor guy—stuck with me."

"Grif was great. He knew all about camp and the programs."

"Impossible." She shoved her plate away. "I've spent seven summers here, and I'm still learning. I was a camper, took the training courses and applied to be a counselor. Now I do all the arts and crafts. JB hired Grif last week, after a counselor got hurt and there was a job opening. I don't know much about him. Some of the counselors have a crush on him, already."

I felt my face burn and changed the topic. "What happened to the counselor who left?" I imagined some creepy creature dragging a body into the bushes.

Tasha looked around, then lowered her voice. "He fell off the plank walk in the Treasure Island Obstacle Course. Had to be airlifted out and flown to the mainland hospital. It was the first bad accident that's happened at camp. Ever. Didn't you hear about it on the news?"

I shook my head. "If there's no technology or phones, how do you know what's going on?"

"We can call home once a week. My parents freaked out when they heard about Ravi's accident. The local media made a huge deal out of it. They implied negligence by JB and the staff. Some people wanted to shut camp down. Afterwards, JB ordered an investigation and held a staff meeting. No one knows why it happened. It happened at night, and Ravi was alone, against camp policy. Now, we constantly review safety procedures. We're lucky Grif was available."

The café door opened and Grif entered with one of his campers in tow—Big-Boy, from the ferry. The boy caught my eye and hesitated. His face was pale, and he seemed nervous. Grif waved at me and my face burned.

Tasha lowered her eyes and pierced the yolk of a poached egg with her knife. Yellow goo leaked over her plate and she swirled her sausage in it. Grif and Big-Boy joined our table with full breakfast trays. Big-Boy didn't talk. He hunched over his plate of fresh fruit and cheese slices and ignored us.

Grif did all the talking. His voice was the only thing I was able to focus on.

"Morning happy campers! There's a busy day ahead of us. The ferry's running nonstop. I saw some black clouds over the lake, though. Might be a storm coming."

People wandered in and all the tables filled up. Tasha introduced me to some other people, then focused on her plate and went quiet. My words stuck in my throat like globs of peanut-butter, and I couldn't speak.

When Tasha pushed her chair back, and said we should leave, I was relieved.

"See you guys around!" Grif waved, then he and Big-Boy headed to the serving area for second helpings.

I scratched the mosquito bite on my wrist and watched Grif saunter away. A flaming red patch spread along the inside of my arm.

Tasha's eyebrows knotted and she whispered, "Leave that

alone. You'll only make things worse."

Did she mean the bite, or Grif?

I wanted to ask Tasha if she needed help, but didn't want to offend her. Most of the camp's spider web of pathways were paved, and she easily maneuvered each twist and turn.

Grif's weather forecast was right. Overhead, fat dark clouds collected, and thunder rumbled over the lake. Before we reached Bobcat cabin, drops of rain landed on our heads and shoulders, so we hurried. By the time we reached the bottom of the ramp, Tasha was out of breath. We paused, and Tasha waved me over.

"Okay, I need a push."

I grabbed the handles at the back of her chair and shoved. When we reached the screen porch and looked across the camp grounds, it was pouring.

"Crap." Tasha pressed the automatic opener for the cabin door and headed for the bathroom. "I wanted to take you to the waterfront, but the path over there isn't paved. It'll be too muddy for me. Check out the activities to figure out what you want to do. You can try something for a day, but after the first three days, there's no switching."

While she got organized, I checked the list we had to submit to Kirra. I picked: Morning—Dance, Yoga. Afternoon – Art, Swim/Waterfront/Free time. There'd be time left over to write in my journal, or figure out how to get off Rainbow Island. The sooner, the better.

It was still raining when we were ready to leave. We both put on raincoats and grabbed umbrellas from a white plastic bucket at the cabin door. Tasha's umbrella hooked into a special holder, but she had trouble with the extra gear and didn't want to get soaked. So, instead of exploring like she'd promised, we headed back to the cafe building. Between meals, it turned into a multi-purpose room.

The other campers and counselors were already inside, playing silly 'get to know you' games. Two senior counselors had set up the craft tables, and put out puzzles and decks of cards. A group had gathered around Ash and Moe, watching Ash juggle plastic cups. Tasha went to the craft table and organized glass jars of coloured beads and lengths of cord.

"This is a great time to make necklaces and bracelets," she said. "I've got tons of materials. Come on, you can make some jewelry."

I checked out the materials she'd collected. Besides the beads, there were jars filled with tiny shells, buttons, feathers and dried flowers. She'd sorted strips of leather and jute and laid out samples of knots to practice tying. I took a container of tiny clay stars and shook pieces into my hand. Before I could string them, someone came from behind and tapped my shoulder.

"Still want to see the waterfront?"

I turned around to see Grif grinning at me.

Obviously annoyed by the interruption, Tasha crossed her arms and leaned back. She already had two of the younger teens at her table slipping coloured glass beads on wire for their bracelets.

"Grif—you'll have to go with her. I'm real busy here and it's too wet. Okay, Raven?"

"Sorry, Tasha." I tried to keep a straight face, and dropped the stars back in the jar. "We can go together another time."

Then Grif yelled so loud the entire room could hear. "We're heading to the beach! Anyone like to join us?"

No one responded, but Ash dropped a cup, knocked his chair over and yelled, "HA!"

"I get it, Superman. Let's go outside." Moe slipped the harness over Ash's chest. "This is just in case."

Griff stiffened. "Is he going to be okay?"

"Sure." Moe didn't sound very confident.

The four of us went out the door and followed the path to the beach.

WHAT HAPPENED TO VIVA?

~~~~~~~~

The rain slowed to a drizzle as we walked to the waterfront. Grif led the way and I walked beside him. Ash and Moe followed at a distance, or zig-zagged around us. While Moe told jokes to distract him, Ash flapped his hands and muttered. I heard a snap when we got close to the water, as Moe attached the leash.

For the first time, I realized that the camp had an awesome waterfront. I'd been so scared when I arrived on the ferry, I hadn't paid any attention to the setting. A wide, sandy beach with three long wooden docks stretched along the shore. Grif explained the biggest dock was for the mainland ferry and motor boats. The other two docks were for the camp's use. An oversized passenger pontoon boat was tied up at one. Stacked on the beach was the water equipment: an emergency throw ring, and racks of kayaks, canoes, and paddleboards. At one end, in a small grey hut with a red tin roof, was a mini office.

"The first aid supplies and lifejackets are stored inside," Grif said when he noticed where I was looking.

"Wow! What's that?" I tugged on his arm and pointed.

Floating beside the pontoon boat was a huge, white plastic blow-up unicorn. A golden horn projected from its forehead, and rainbow-striped wings extended from its sides. I'd seen inflatable boats before, small ones shaped like flamingos or swans. But this unicorn was mammoth sized. Big enough to hold six people!

Moe threw his head back and laughed. "We call that thing *Pegasus*! It's the most popular boat here. The campers love it. It's not allowed out onto the main part of the lake. It's not sturdy enough for the waves and deep water—it's also hard to steer. It's a toy for the beach area."

I caught my breath. I didn't know how to paddle a canoe or kayak, but the unicorn was fantastic. In my mind, I imagined a new plan.

If I snuck away at night, I could take the unicorn and leave by floating across the lake to the mainland. Then I'd make a new life for myself. Somehow. I just hadn't figured out the 'somehow'. But what a way to escape!

Ash interrupted my running-away fantasy. His hands flapped, then he tugged on the leash like he wanted to run. Moe tried to help him.

"It's just the water making waves," he said to Ash. "That's why you hear splashing."

When heavy waves from a passing wakeboarder battered the sides of the boats tied at the dock and swooshed against the shore, Ash's anxiety increased. He made sounds that weren't quite words, and pulled harder.

Moe tried to calm him, and said, "That noise is from the boats making the waves. Let's watch them for a while." To help Ash relax, they stepped onto the dock and sat on a pair of red wooden chairs positioned at the end.

"Sweet place, huh?" Grif pointed at the camp's stretch of golden beach. "After the mainland condo development is finished, this'll be a water park. It's big enough for trampolines, slides, pools."

What was he talking about?

I didn't know what to say. Being close to him made me lightheaded, but I wanted him to like me, so I tried to be funny.

"Sure. And maybe a restaurant and swim up bar."

The rain started again, and Grif said we should head back to the cafeteria.

Ash didn't want to leave, so Moe stayed on the dock.

The path from the waterfront was narrow and wet, so Grif and I walked close together. He asked if I'd picked my activities, and seemed happy when I said I'd be at the beach every day.

Halfway back, he stopped, popped a stick of gum in his mouth, then said, "Viva . . . what happened to you?"

That caught me off guard. "What are you talking about?"

"Oh *right* . . . you're using a different name here. *Raven.* You know exactly what I'm talking about. When you sang in the finale of the TripleT show, something happened. When you opened your mouth and squawked like a duck, it was hilarious! And then you squawked again. When you ran off the stage squawking, I laughed so hard I almost pissed myself. I must've watched the video a thousand times."

I was stunned. I wanted to run for the cabin, but my legs were frozen to the ground.

"H-how did you know?"

"I used your photo from yesterday to do a facial recognition. You've changed your name and hair, but it took less than a minute." He squeezed my shoulder and smiled. "Don't worry! Nobody's perfect. We've all done things. Your secret's safe with me . . . I'm a big fan! Loved the way you belted out those old-time songs. Just like your mother used to do when she was a star. What were you supposed to do for the finale?"

"*Somewhere Over the Rainbow*." Tears welled in my eyes, and my throat tightened. "That song's my dad's favourite. I wanted to dedicate it to him."

He patted my shoulder. "It's okay. I won't tell anyone."

It felt like a bucket of icy water had been dumped on me, or I'd gone to school naked. I stood there, trembling and feeling sick.

"Hey—look!" Grif pointed at Ash running full tilt across the field in the direction of the cafeteria. Moe charged after him.

Laughing, Ash yelled over his shoulder, "Lunch time!"

It was the most I'd heard him say. Moe joined him and they headed for the cafeteria.

It started to pour, and we ran too. The scary discussion with Grif was over. For the moment.

THE FIRST RAINBOW

~~~~~~~

After lunch, the last ferry of campers arrived, and everyone moved into their cabins. Tasha was busy greeting and supervising the new people. The regular campers were between twelve and sixteen. Because Bobcat cabin was for LITs, (except me) the girls in my cabin were a bit older—seventeen or eighteen.

None of the others recognized me, and I stuck to the fake story that I'd told Tasha when we did introductions.

The other girls in my cabin gossiped while they unpacked their gear. Their voices were loud and irritating. I was an only child and used to lots of privacy. After what I'd been through, it was difficult to deal with all that energy, so while they organized, I kept to myself.

It was hard to remember all their names. Why bother, anyway? Instead, I gave them nicknames, based on their appearances, or annoying habits.

Mid-afternoon, the rain stopped and the sun came out. As a group, our cabin walked over to the cafe for supper. JB waited outside, ringing a dinner bell that could be heard all over camp. Ash arrived with Moe, without the leash. He was calmer than at the beach, and Moe had fitted him with his red headphones.

The doors to the cafeteria were closed, so everyone collected outside the building. JB climbed onto a small wood platform, then blew a horn. When it was quiet, he pointed at the sky over the waterfront and said, "Look over there."

Wow. In the distance, a huge rainbow glowed over the lake. One end of the arc sank into the water, the other disappeared into the trees on Treasure Island. JB paused long enough for us to appreciate the view. The colours were intense, almost glittering. Distinct bars of red, orange, yellow, green, blue, indigo, violet blurred into each other. After a moment, JB gave a short blast with his horn.

"Helllooooo campers! Welcome to Camp Rainbow Wings. Who's here for the first time?"

Arms raised in the air around me, so I wiggled my fingers.

"A special welcome to the newcomers," JB said. He waved in the direction of the lake. "All the old timers here know that, after a storm, when the sun comes out, there's always a rainbow over there. Sometimes two. You just have to look."

JB took off his bowler hat and rubbed his forehead with the back of his hand. "After supper, we have another tradition. Tonight, our first campfire program is . . . the Counselor Showcase!"

Like they'd turned into a pack of wolves, the senior counselors howled, and the campers clapped and whistled.

JB threw his hat in the hair, then ducked so it landed on his head. "Now, who's hungry?"

The cafeteria doors swung open and there was a stampede to get inside. It was chaos in the room until we found our table groups.

Tasha gestured at my cabin mates and said, "Let's go quick. Grab the table by the wall. The Bobcats always sit together for meals." We got to the table and pulled up the chairs. Everyone started talking at once. The noise was massive. I still couldn't remember anyone's name, but I started to notice their differences. One girl had a high-pitched voice, another one continually tossed her long blond hair, another was bossy, one wore glasses. Their energy was overwhelming.

The LITs had been campers at Rainbow Wings before, and knew how things worked. Listening to them, I learned a lot about the camp, including that it tried to be environmentally friendly.

The girl-with-glasses (I named her Spex) informed me that one of the activity choices was Gardening. The camp grew its own vegetables and used them for meals. The biggest challenge was to keep animals out of the garden. The deer also got their food at camp!

"Yuck. I don't want to look for bugs and pull weeds. These fingernails cost me a fortune." I displayed my hands to show that I'd just had a manicure.

No one talked to me for the rest of the meal.

Some of the campers who'd come over on my ferry ride were helping in the kitchen. They'd made lasagna—meat or veggie. Also green salad and home-made buns. Peach pie for dessert. Tasha said that their supervisor, the man with the waxed moustache, had given up working in a in a four-star restaurant to live and work at camp. Everyone just called him Cook. Super original.

At 7:00 P.M. we headed to the fire pit area for evening assembly. As soon as we left the cafeteria, I could smell the campfire smoke. I hoped the stench wouldn't stick to my hair.

It was a short walk past the other cabins and across the sports field. The Bobcats stayed together in a tight, cliquey group. The girl with the annoying voice was the only one who talked to me. In my head I named her 'Squeak'.

"I've seen you somewhere before," she said.

"Doubt it. We all have a ... whatchamacallit—" I turned my face away.

"A doppelganger." Rapunzel (the girl with long hair) was eavesdropping. She flipped her hair off her shoulders. "Everyone says I'm just like Elsa from Frozen."

"Totally!" Apparently Squeak was also a suck-up.

Tasha had gone ahead of us, so I left them behind, and joined her at the camp fire.

Wooden benches were set into a crescent shape hill, with a flat open area at the bottom for the fire pit and performers. A pile of logs blazed in the centre, and red and orange flames shot out in all directions, and sent sparks into the air. It wasn't quite dark. Fading clouds of pink and yellow hung overhead. Long shadows stretched from the fire into the crowd.

JB stood brace-legged in the middle of it all, until everyone arrived and took their seats. Then, he blew his horn and waited for quiet.

"Helloooooo . . ."

"Helloooooo . . ." the crowd yelled back on the cue.

He practiced a few more group echoes, and the counselors and campers both knew what he expected and replied.

"How are you? Good to see you!"

"Where are the Bobcats?"

"Where are the Moose?"

"Where are the Bears?"

Without missing a cue, the cabin group and their counselor answered him every time. Some of the cabin groups made animal noises and did goofy actions. They were loud and funny. The acoustics were terrific, as clear and sharp as if JB had a mic and amplifier.

JB removed his bowler and sat on a stool, legs sprawled out in front. He didn't raise his voice, but I heard every word. Despite his cheesy appearance and corny speech, he was as polished as any show host I'd ever worked with.

He stood and raised his hand to recite an Indigenous Land Acknowledgement. After a pause for respect, he pointed to the audience.

"This afternoon, the sky held a rainbow . . . and there's a rainbow with us tonight. Many different people come to Rainbow Island. And each person belongs. At Camp Rainbow Wings, it doesn't matter how you look, how smart you are, how strong you are, or how much money your parents have."

With his right hand in a fist, he limped up to where we sat on the benches, and raised his voice. "What *does matter* is who you are. Be kind . . . be honest . . . that's what matters. Together we'll make a beautiful rainbow."

It was a mushy speech, but the way JB spoke, with his gruff, raspy voice . . . it felt real. It felt honest. Everyone was quiet. He called out the question that he'd asked me earlier.

"What sound does a rainbow make?"

The campers yelled out dumb stuff.

"Yellow!"

"Green!"

"Oink oink."

"Quack quack!"

The kids laughed and punched each other.

JB laughed and slapped his leg with his bowler.

"Nope. I'm still waiting for the right answer. One day, someone will know." He put his hat back on and raised his voice. "And now, for a special treat, I give you . . . only at Camp Rainbow Wings . . . The tremendous . . . *TOWER OF POWER!*"

Into the centre of the circle came the senior counselors. Moe simultaneously rode a unicycle and juggled tennis balls. A girl with braided hair did flips and cartwheels. One guy walked on stilts. A band played as a trio of girls sang feel-good cover songs. Tasha was the lead vocal, and she was good. No, not good. She was awesome.

I watched from a log bench beside the Bobcat cabin girls. Spex leaned over and whispered, "Aren't they amazing? This always happens the first night of camp. Next year, I'll be a senior counselor. I'm a gymnast."

Half-way through a song, JB joined the band with his guitar. It turned into an old-fashioned sing-a-long. They sang songs I'd learned as a little kid, plus new ones. Funny, sentimental, repeat-o-style, with hand and body motions. And the classics. Even 'Kumbaya'. We waved our hands in the air, clapped, and stomped our feet.

Automatically, I opened my mouth and sang.

When my voice faltered and squawked, Spex shot me a dirty look.

After the last song, the crowd broke into wild cheers and clapped. JB went back to his stool and waited, one hand up, until it was quiet. When he pulled a red ball out of his pocket and popped it on his nose, I cringed.

The senior counselors came through the audience, and handed each of us a canvas goodie bag stamped with the camp logo. I opened mine and winced. Inside was a white t-shirt and a red-nose ball.

Tasha stuck the ball on her nose and crossed her eyes. "After breakfast tomorrow, we'll make our own tie-dye camp shirts," she said.

BWaaaaahp! JB blew into his clown horn. "Because this is the last camp session this summer, we've planned a special program for the parent performance. The theme is . . ." he paused and we all held our breath.

" PIRATES! Shiver me timbers!"

The campers and counselors screamed, "Pirates!"

JB raised his fist and bellowed, "ARRRRR!"

The audience stood up, raised their fists and echoed. "ARRRRR!"

"ARRRRR!"

The roaring echo continued, until my ears ached, but I laughed.

When it was over, one voice yelled, "ARRRRR!" over and over until the crowd shushed him. Of course, it was Ash. He jumped, spun around and yelled, "ARRRR!"

Moe stood beside him and waited until he calmed. He took Ash's hand, then adjusted his headphones and helped him sit on a bench.

By then, it was dark. As the fire burned to coals, the camp band played their last song. The drummer's solo started with a basic rock and roll pattern. In the middle, he increased the tempo and added tom-toms and the hi-hat. The volume diminished and the tension built.

Thump-thump, thump-thump, thump-thump. Like a heartbeat. Then the noise crescendoed. For the finale, he smashed his sticks against the cymbals.

CRASH!

The sound bounced and echoed back from the waterfront. It was a good way to end the evening. The crowd whistled and clapped. We climbed down the hillside and headed for the cabins. Across the open areas, the dark forest stretched, and the mosquitos swarmed.

It was scary, and for the first time since coming to camp, I was glad to be with a group. We'd almost arrived at Bobcat cabin when we heard pounding footsteps and panting breath behind us.

The dining hall bell clanged in the distance.

Tasha lifted her hand and we stood still. "That's the alarm bell. That means there's an emergency."

Wild-eyed and gasping for breath, Moe appeared out of the dark with the leash dangling in his hand.

"Have you seen Ash?"

RUN AWAY

~~~~~~~~~~~~~

"What happened? How'd you lose him?" Tasha sounded mad—and scared.

Moe's words came out in bursts as he gasped for breath. He sounded panicky and defensive.

"He did great during the assembly, so I didn't want to use his tether. He was having fun and loved the pirate stuff. But he got too excited. When the cymbal smashed, he jumped in the air and yelled, 'Crocodiles!' Then he took off."

"Which way?" Tasha's voice was frantic. "That poor kid. He could get lost. Or drown! JB's ringing the alarm. We have to search our areas."

"I'm supposed to check around the cafeteria. As long as he

didn't go into the woods . . ." Moe swiveled and sprinted away.

I had a funny feeling that I knew where Ash had gone. "I bet he went to the beach. We were there earlier and he liked it there."

Tasha nodded. "That's a good possibility, but I can't go there. It's not in my search area. The LITs can help me check behind the cabins. The waterfront is someone else's area, but go ahead and check."

I was scared already, but then Tasha made it worse when she said, "Be careful!"

Of what? Did she know something I didn't? All my fears from the night before flooded back. My stomach twisted into a pretzel.

There was enough glow from the solar lights on the paths to show the way to the beach. When I arrived at the waterfront, there was a crowd of people huddled on the edge of the camp dock. From somewhere in the middle of them, I heard Grif shout, "Hey kid... get outta there! You gotta go back to your cabin!"

Then I saw Ash—and I felt sick.

He'd climbed inside Pegasus and was on his knees, rocking and muttering. The inflatable boat had been left high up on the beach, but the wind was strong, and waves splashed against it. I wasn't sure what to do. It was horrible to watch, but it was impossible to look away. When Grif and his boys screamed at Ash, it didn't help. It made things worse.

Once, my dad had a student in his class who had meltdowns. I remembered what he'd told me. *I have to give them time and space. Stay calm and help them relax. Let them know they're safe.*

I remembered something else. My therapist had suggested a strategy to use when I was stressed out. Like a cop at a street crossing, I held up my hand to stop the yelling on the dock, then closed my eyes and slowly counted to ten. She was right. It helped me focus.

I headed towards the unicorn, trying to keep my voice steady.

"Ash, do you remember me? I'm your friend, Raven. I'm just walking up to you. If that's okay." My throat was croaky, still sore from the campfire sing-a-long. I tried again. "Remember in the office, you showed me how you could catch things? You were amazing." The rocking slowed, and he was quiet. I patted the unicorn's wing and tried to keep my voice calm.

"Ash, what's up, buddy?"

He didn't respond, so I squatted on the sand near him. "I'm here," I said. "I'll wait until you're ready."

Nothing happened.

A boy at the dock yelled, "Hurry up! The bugs out here are killing me. I want to get back to the cabin."

Grif hollered, "Settle down. She's doing a great job." The complaining stopped, and Grif took charge. "She's got things under control. Go find Moe and JB and tell them he's on the beach. Then head to the cabin and get to bed. I'll wait here until they're ready to leave."

"Are you okay now, Ash?" He flinched when I touched his shoulder, so I pulled my hand away. "When the drummer hit that cymbal, it was pretty scary. Made me jump—it scared me, too."

He shifted away and turned his head to the side. "Superman's not scared. Pirates! ARRRRR! The scurvy dogs . . . the scurvy dogs . . ." He pointed across the open water. "Stay away!"

"ARRR!" I stood beside him and raised my fist. "Go back, you worthless scum!"

He dropped his arm to his side and stared at me. I hoped that I sounded calmer than I felt.

"It's okay, Ash. All the pirates are gone. It's safe. Let's go to your cabin. Moe's looking for you." I held out my hand and he took it. His fingers were cold and stiff.

Grif walked with us towards the cabins. Nobody spoke, but

it felt good to be with Grif, like things were safe. Ahead, there were voices and bobbing flashlights. Moe appeared and shone a light in our eyes. Ash winced and stiffened. I thought he was going to run.

"It's okay, Ash," I said. He held onto my hand and crouched on the path. I sat beside him. Grif pushed against Moe's shoulder.

"Stick the leash back on this kid." Grif sounded angry. "It's your fault he took off, Moe. He could have drowned, you idiot."

Moe ignored Grif. He got on his knees beside Ash and said, "Come on, Superman. It's safe now. The pirates are gone. This was all my fault. Let's go to the cabin."

"Okay."

Ash got up and walked away with Moe. I waited with Grif until we couldn't see their flashlight bobbing ahead of us on the path. Grif was still angry.

"This camp's a joke, and that kid's the worst of the bunch. That stupid idiot Moe almost lost him. If the news gets out, this place is in even worse trouble."

I didn't understand. How Grif talked about the kids made my skin crawl, but then I figured he was just upset and worried. The way he was acting reminded me of the stage manager at TripleT. He'd be so uptight about the show, he'd yell at people. Afterwards, he was always apologetic.

Maybe Grif was just worried. It would help him to talk about things.

"What do you mean, worse trouble?" I asked.

"The camp's going bust. JB's in serious financial trouble. He won't be able to hold out much longer. If he wasn't too stubborn to sell, this place could be turned into a great resort."

Shoulder to shoulder, we silently walked to the Bobcat cabin. In the darkness around us, I heard hoots, rustles, chirping. Again,

I was glad I wasn't alone.

Tasha had left the porch light on.

When we arrived, Grif moved closer and lowered his voice.

"That was a tough start to your start at camp, Raven. Sometimes I'm a jerk and say things I shouldn't. Sorry—I want to do a good job here. I'll admit that I'm not perfect. You were great with him."

He put a hand on my shoulder and squeezed. "And don't worry, I'll keep your secrets. I checked the waterfront schedule and sign-up sheets, and saw your name. See you tomorrow."

DYE OR DROWN – WHICH IS WORSE?

~~~~~~~~

At sunrise the next morning, everyone was still asleep in Bobcat cabin—except me. I had been asleep until the girl I named 'Rip' snored. And she kept snoring. It began as a drawn out '*Ronc!*' then turned into a '*shshsh*'. Her snores sounded like a ripsaw. I wanted to smother her with my pillow.

But I didn't. At that moment, I didn't want to add the title of 'Teen Murderer' to my already ruined reputation.

As I lay sleepless in my bunk, a loop played on repeat in my mind.

Last night with Grif.

What happened? He'd apologized for losing his cool. But later . . . was he just a super friendly guy, or was he flirting?

61

I took my journal out and tried to sort things out. At our last session, my therapist suggested it would help me to write. It felt different than texting, I had to organize my thoughts into longer sentences. I drew pictures instead of using emojis.

Once, as a joke, Dr. Hill had suggested that I write a book about my life. When I laughed, she said, "I predict it could be a *New York Times* Bestseller!"

Could she have predicted what happened after breakfast?

It started off okay. I'd already picked a full schedule for the day. Dance, Yoga, Swimming... but the first activity after breakfast was to tie-dye my camp shirt.

Tasha set out big plastic buckets and spray bottles filled with coloured dye along the sports field. The entire camp turned out for what JB had said would be a 'bonding experience.'

Let's not forget he promised it would be fun.

First, we took our new camp shirts out of the bags, and used elastics to tie knotted bundles all over them. We were supposed to put on gloves, soak the shirts in clean water, then dip the knots into the buckets of coloured dyes, or spray them. Tasha told us to lay the shirts in the sun to dry, then rinse out the dye and wear them at events.

The clean water soak was fine, until for fun, one of Grif's kids grabbed the hose and sprayed him. Grif lost his temper, swore and took the hose. Then the rest of the Bear cabin boys tackled him, seized the hose and sprayed random people.

Everyone ran around, laughing and knocking over the buckets of dye. The Bobcat LITs tried to wrestle the hose away, and stepped on the finished t-shirts that were spread out on the grass to dry. Ash got excited, and Moe had to calm him. I tried to spray my shirt before the dye ran out, but forgot to put on gloves.

It ended when JB blasted his horn.

After we cleaned up, I glanced at my hands.

Blue! No matter how much I scrubbed, they stayed the colour of a cartoon monster. I looked like the Disney genie who escaped Aladdin's lamp. Or a Smurf.

Then it was time to go to our first class.

Eight other campers joined me on the stage for dance class. An senior counselor named Willa, was our instructor. She had long hair, long legs and big boobs, and it looked like she'd had dance training.

Willa said we'd practice basic dance steps for the first week, then later, when she found the right tune, we'd rehearse numbers for the finale.

"It's impossible to find decent pirate music." After she saw my blue hands, she tried to be funny. "Gurl, this isn't supposed to be a horror show."

After dance class, the amazing and beautiful Willa also led the Yoga class.

"Let's take the mats to the dock and do our practice by the water," she said.

Exhausted from being awake all night, I stumbled along behind the group like a sleepwalker. Willa told us to place our mats on the dock and relax on them. As I lay down, a jet boat went by on the lake, with music playing from its speakers. The sun was hot. I fell asleep.

Willa woke me when class was over.

Then it was back to the cafeteria for lunch. When we rehearsed at TripleT, food trucks catered our meals, so I'd become used to standing in a lineup to choose my meals. It was usually top quality, fresh market food. Now I picked Chili dogs and a bag of potato chips.

At the Bobcat table, I noticed a girl in our cabin who didn't eat much. She'd brought a pair of chopsticks from home, and just pushed food around with them. A napkin hid the remaining food on her plate when she finished.

Anorexia? I'd seen that before. Inside my head, I named her, 'Stix.' The others talked about their classes while I picked kidney beans out of the chili. I hated kidney beans almost as much as onions. I didn't pay attention to their conversations until Tasha announced to everyone at the table that I was on my school's swim team.

I choked on a piece of lettuce. Squeak and Rip pounded my back.

Thankfully, the others weren't going to the beach in the afternoon. I hoped they wouldn't find out that I could barely float.

After the LITs left for their afternoon activities, Tasha set out the supplies for the Arts and Crafts classes. She wanted me to help brainstorm and sketch ideas for the SHIVERS! set and costumes.

This is such amateur stuff, I thought. *Why don't they hire a decent set designer?*

The highlight of the day came later when I had a few moments alone in the cabin. Before I'd left, Suzi'd bought me a hot pink bikini and matching floral print towel. I'd discovered it at the bottom of my suitcase when I'd unpacked. It was perfect for lying on the beach and working on my tan. She'd also bought me a pair of pink espadrilles with wedge heels. My hands were still blue, but at least the bikini and shoes matched my nail polish!

If I drowned while learning to swim, at least I'd look good when they hauled the body in.

ANOTHER LITTLE SECRET

~~~~~~~

When I arrived at the beach that afternoon, it was already crowded with noisy campers. Swimming and boating were popular choices for afternoon activities. The shallow end of the waterfront was marked off with floating green and white buoys. A senior counselor wearing a floppy hat and red t-shirt sat on the lifeguard tower.

I spotted Grif immediately, as he walked around supervising the swimmers. He was a magnet—I couldn't pull my eyes away. His tanned bare chest, lean muscles, handsome face . . . the best-looking guy on the beach *and* he was funny. When he joked around or splashed them, everyone laughed.

Before we were allowed go in the water, we had to pass a swimming test. Camp rules. Twenty kids waited on the dock for their turn. My gut twisted as I watched them and tried to figure out what to do. If I failed the test, they'd all know that I'd lied about being on the school team.

To pass the test, we had to do a short swim between the two camp docks. Wrapped in my new towel, I stood at the dock's edge, and watched the others jump in and splash across the gap.

The spectators on the dock yelled, "*GO! GO! GO!*"

It didn't take much time to get across. When they finished, the swimmers climbed a ladder and waited on the other dock. Each time someone finished, they all clapped and cheered.

When I was a little kid, my dad had taken me for Parent and Tot swim lessons. He'd stand in the pool, arms outstretched, then I'd plug my nose and jump. He'd catch me, and we'd bounce up and down yelling *Wheee!* We'd duck underwater and jump up, into the air. At first, it felt like I was flying. *Wheee!* He showed me how to put my face in the water and blow bubbles. That's as far as we got. I swallowed a mouthful of water and choked. I panicked, and never learned to float. Even with dad holding me, I was too scared.

Then I started performing with Suzi, and life got too busy with piano and voice lessons. I hadn't gone near water for years.

"Your turn." Grif pointed at me. "Jump in and swim across." I felt all the eyes on me. Like—*do or die.* It was *exactly* like when I first stepped onto the stage. I dropped my towel, gulped a mouthful of air, plugged my nose, and jumped.

Yikes! It took my breath away. The water was cold. So cold it burned. I heard an explosion and rising air bubbles. My feet hit the muck at the bottom. I bounced back up to the surface, gulped some air and grabbed a board at the edge of the dock. The water wasn't deep, just a bit over my head. Worst-case scenario, I could bounce my way across.

By splashing my arms and kicking hard, I got across without

drowning. It was a miracle. I grabbed the edge of the dock and pulled myself over to the ladder. When I climbed the metal rungs, the other swimmers clapped and cheered. *Wheee!* It wasn't a real swim, but it felt good. Real good.

Like old times, I struck a pose, and bowed.

We had an hour to swim, and after running in and out of the water, and jumping off the dock a few times, I stretched out on my towel where I had a good view of the swimmers, and soaked up the sun. I decided to try canoeing next.

I watched Grif put his hands under a girl's back to help her float. When they finished, she squealed and splashed him. He did a beautiful jack-knife dive off the diving board, then had a big water fight with the younger boys. They all loved him.

At the end of the session, the dinner bell clanged. I slid on my pink espadrilles, grabbed my towel and headed up the path towards Bobcat cabin.

Someone came up behind me and bumped a shoulder against mine. Grif.

"You *don't* know how to swim, do you?"

How did he know? My face burned. I didn't know what to say.

"I saw you touch the bottom. Half-way across, you bounced and touched down again. In fact, you did that a lot. You walked in the middle section. You should've failed the swim test, but I didn't want to embarrass you. You'll be in big trouble if you have to swim any distance. How 'bout I give you some private lessons? It would just be another little secret between us."

I chewed on my bottom lip. We had too many secrets already. I had a bad feeling—this could lead to other things I shouldn't do. I decided to say no.

My eyes met his, and he gave me a thumbs up signal. My knees wobbled and I felt sick.

"Sure!" I said. "When?"

"How 'bout during the free block? I'll get some time off. We can meet at the beach."

"Deal."

We separated, and I headed to Bobcat cabin, with my stomach twisting. When I arrived, Tasha was waiting outside. Her arms were crossed, and she treated me like she was a drill sergeant.

"Where have you been? I thought you'd be back before this. Is there anything we should discuss?"

"Everything was great! Loved the beach. I've decided to do extra swimming . . ."

"Right." Her tone was sarcastic. She pushed ahead to our cabin and opened the door. "That's because you're the star of your school's swim team . . ."

I followed her inside. Squeak was ironing her camp t-shirt while the other four played cards at the big table. They glanced up and waved, then went back to their game.

Tasha motioned me closer and whispered, "Raven—tonight, after campfire assembly, you and I are gonna have a chat."

YELL IF YOU NEED HELP

~~~~~~~~

During supper, JB blew his horn for attention to remind us about the evening program. "It's cooling off outside. Wear a hoodie and long pants tonight. Moe's got an *amaaaaazzzing* surprise!"

We went back to Bobcat cabin to change. I was grateful to my mother for buying me cute matching grey yoga-pants and a fleece hoodie. Shopping was Suzi's strength. When I stepped outside the cabin with the other girls, it was windy, and the air smelt smoky. JB was right. The temperature had dropped. I shivered and went back for my jean jacket while they waited on the path.

On the walk over, Tasha explained the night's campfire program. '*Testimonials,*' she called it. It was traditional for two or three of the senior counselors to tell their personal stories, and how they'd struggled with a challenge. She said they'd talk about their fears, failures and successes. Traumas, family issues, health problems—whatever. Tasha said it was a good way for us to make connections with each other. A way to build trust.

When all the campers had gathered, a few senior counsellors shared their stories.

When it was Tasha's turn, the wheel of her chair got stuck at the bottom of the ramp and Grif helped her get to the platform.

Tasha talked about her life before and after the accident. Classic Tasha. She said that over time, she'd learned to do almost anything she wanted. But I knew that some of what she said was just brave talk. Up close, I'd seen the strain on her face when things were hard—or impossible—for her. With the help of the LITs, I'd already learned to assist her in our modified bathroom.

Because he was new, Grif was asked to introduce himself. He talked about his life-long goal to play pro basketball. It had seemed like it was coming true, then he'd broken his leg in a tournament. He felt responsible when his team lost. Because of the injury, he'd failed his first year of college.

He was so sincere; my heart went out to him.

Rapunzel and Spex sat beside me. As the program went on, they wiped away tears. Kids near me hugged each other.

I didn't move. My cynical mind saw through the intent of the program's set-up. We were supposed to feel inspired—connected to each other by our common problems.

Yeah, right.

No one's situation felt as bad as *mine*.

Who else's life had been destroyed by social media? As the love-in continued, ugly memories flooded back. I stopped listening to the speakers, scratched my mosquito bites until they bled and thought about my miserable life.

70

At first, being a child entertainer was fun. Especially performing with my mom. Once my personal career became successful, I worked hard every day to be perfect. When I made the TripleT finals, and got the chance to win a million dollars, I practiced harder, and longer. For hours and hours. But after a while, my throat felt sore and dry. The sound was hoarse and rough. It got worse, so I worked harder.

Then, in the final show, with all the pressure on me, my vocal cords snapped. I squawked. On stage. In front of all the cameras. Total humiliation.

I ran off the stage squawking, and collapsed behind the curtain. The crew called an ambulance, and I was hospitalized. The doctors said I'd had a vocal hemorrhage. Like Adele did. And long ago, a singer named Julie Andrews, from "The Sound of Music."

When I was released, every place I went, I was photographed. The worst pictures were shared online and laughed about.

'Baby fat teen star eats entire pizza!'

'Did she swallow a gerbil or a pig?'

'Viva Tantie – is she an alien love child?'

Funny? NO!

On-line threats and hate mail arrived. Lots of it. I was terrified, but couldn't stay away from social media. It became an addiction. That's when I started scratching. The pain in my arm distracted me from the pain in my heart.

At home, my mom was too busy with work to notice me falling apart. And she and my dad fought. Life was a nightmare.

I was a loser . . . and decided they'd be better off without me.

The TripleT management released a fake story to the media. They said I'd used a 'health restoring' remedy I'd discovered on the internet to fix my voice. The ingredients were "accidently" mixed and backfired.

Liars. No one believed them anyway.

The health restoring recipe? Mix two common household ingredients, and gargle. It was supposed to destroy bacteria, whiten my teeth, and fix my ruined vocal cords.

I didn't gargle. I swallowed.

The mix was deadly.

Suzi came home late and found me passed out on the kitchen floor.

Back to the hospital I went for treatment, followed by months of staying home. I was ordered not to speak. Even a whisper could make the damage worse.

Okay. Enough. From the centre of the campfire circle, JB's horn blast crashed my pity-party and brought me back to reality.

The senior counselor's stories were finished. I saw the Bobcat girls' tears and heard sniffles and sobs in the audience around me. JB asked for a group hug.

"The world's biggest!" He stretched out his arms and the campers ran down the hillside and gathered around the platform. It felt like I was carried along in a swarm of bees.

After the massive love in, JB shouted, "It's 'Fabulous Fun' time! Come on . . . Moe's set it up, and I want everyone join in!"

"Let's do it!" the counselors shouted.

After high-fiving us, the counselors distributed pails of soap solution, and wands with circular rings on the ends. When they dipped the wands in the liquid and swirled them around, long bubble tunnels appeared. Childish, I thought.

As they held the wands overhead and ran, transparent tubes of colour drifted behind them. Like they'd transformed into cosmic spirits, light from the fire shimmered on the surface of the soap bubbles.

"Bubbles! Run!" Ash charged by me with a long river of bubble flowing alongside him.

Moe ran close behind him and yelled, "Great job, Superman! Run faster!"

Grif walked by, then stood beside me, grinning like it was all a big joke. "He's let that nut bar off the leash again. Moe's not only a lousy rapper, he's stupid."

His words made me uncomfortable, but I nodded and Grif pointed at another group. "Check out those idiots. Acting like a bunch of preschoolers."

His Bear cabin campers were messing with the other kids' wands and trying to pop their bubble streams. Big-boy ran behind Ash and Moe until he was out of breath and had to stop.

When the buckets were empty, Tasha collected the wands. The wind felt colder, so I buttoned my jacket and put up the collar. Everyone heard JB blow his horn and we headed back to the benches. Moe dumped more wood on the campfire.

CRACK! From somewhere in the woods outside the camp property there was a loud snap. It sounded like a gun-shot. It was followed by a drawn-out whoosh, then crackling noises as branches broke. Then *THUMP*.

Whatever it was, it hit the ground so hard, everything shook.

A senior counsellor yelled, "It was just a tree falling."

One of the younger campers hollered, "Moe! That guy just took off!"

I knew who it had to be.

Ash had run away again.

JB's smile disappeared. Head down, he limped to the camp bell and rang it over and over. Moe and Cook made the campers sit in place. When it was quiet, the senior counselors ordered us to stay seated at the campfire while they searched their designated areas.

Before they left, Grif grabbed Moe's arm—in front of the entire camp—and shook him.

"You friggin' idiot! Why didn't you keep him on the leash?"

Moe pushed Grif away but looked shaken and unsteady.

"Check the beach!" One of the Bear campers pointed at the waterfront. "That's where he went last time."

Moe bolted and Grif charged after him. I tried to follow them, but Tasha grabbed my arm.

"Stop!" She tugged me closer and said, "I saw Ash leave. I think he ran into the woods . . . into the old sanctuary area. There's a dirt path between the trees. I can take you to the entrance, but I can't manage the rest. You'll have to go alone.

"I can't . . . it's getting dark! I don't have a flashlight!"

"Neither does he."

"But I'm scared—"

The message in her brown eyes shut me up. *Wimp.*

Tasha shoved and strained to get across the bumpy field, and I followed. When it got too rough and she started to swear, I pushed. At the edge of the woods, under a *No Trespassing* sign, we stopped to catch our breath. We were both panting and sweaty.

After a minute, she pointed out a faint trail between the trees. "I'm positive he ran over there. He couldn't have gone far. He's probably hiding close by. Stay on the path, and yell if you find him or need help."

RUN AWAY AGAIN

~~~~~~~~

There wasn't going to be any 'friendly' chat with Tasha tonight; she'd obviously forgotten about being pissed off at me earlier. This was an opportunity to prove I wasn't all bad, but I was still scared.

Without glancing back at her, I stumbled along the trail. Low branches whacked me and scratched my face. I tried to keep calm. *He couldn't have gone far. He doesn't have a flashlight. He's not wearing a coat. He'll be cold and frightened.* My head pounded as the thoughts raced through my brain.

It was like hearing my father talk to me, telling me what to do. Feeling braver, I called into the woods.

"Ash! Where are you?"

No answer, so I kept moving forward. It was after sunset, but there was a faint afterglow in the sky, and I could see a little way ahead. Something in the bushes snapped. I shivered and wanted to turn around. If I went any deeper into the forest, it would be too dark to see. I called again.

"Ash! It's me—Raven, your friend! Where are you?"

He still didn't answer.

I swore and swatted a mosquito off my neck. My whole body strained to listen. All around me, invisible creatures rustled in the bushes. Crickets chirped. In the distance, an owl hooted. My skin prickled, and I wanted to scream. I had an eerie feeling something dangerous was crouched nearby.

Before camp, I'd always lived in the city and had a weird paranoia of the woods. I worried about wild animals like bears and wolves. In this place, there might even be a cougar. What if there were animals that hunted in the dark? A twig snapped.

My heart hammered, and I couldn't move. Then it was dead silent.

"Ash? Is that you?

No response. I called again.

"Help." His voice was weak, but not far ahead. Step by step, I crept forward, arms stretched out in front to push the branches away.

"It's okay, Ash. That *was* a creepy sound. It scared *everyone*. It was just a broken tree hitting the ground. Nothing to hurt you."

"A tree—"

"Ash . . . It's late. *Please* stand up, and come out to the trail where I can see you. JB wants to teach us a song about pirates tonight. Come on, Superman, let's go back."

"Not Superman. Ash is a pirate! ARRRRRR!"

"Yes! ARRRRR! Yes . . . we're both pirates! Come out, Brave Pirate, and lead me to camp."

A few yards ahead, just off the trail, something moved. I froze. Then, covered with broken twigs and pine needles, Ash crawled out from a pile of brush. When he reached the path, he stopped and sat, head down, arms wrapped around his knees.

I wanted to hug him, but hesitated when I got close. He didn't like to be touched, especially when he was upset. Instead, I sat on the dirt beside him and waited. "You okay?"

He didn't respond.

Now what? A little ahead of us, beneath the leaves at the side of the path, there was a rustle. My skin prickled, and I tensed. *What was that? A rattlesnake?*

Ash lifted his head and crawled forward, trying to see what it was. I wanted to turn and run, but where?

"Ash . . . don't go!"

It was too late—he'd disappeared. There was no choice but to follow him, so I did—feeling my way on hands and knees, cursing at the rocks and branches. As I got close, I smelt the stink of his BO.

My nose was almost in his butt, so when he abruptly stopped, we crashed and fell. He pointed to a quivering shape half-hidden beneath a broken branch. "Stuck—"

"Don't touch it!"

"Stuck . . . stuck! Raven . . . help."

"What are you talking about? We gotta get outta here—"

"Bird." Ash pointed. "Stuck."

He was right. It was hard to see, but something was trapped, flopping in the leaves. We crawled closer. When I lifted the branch away, Ash knelt, stretched his hands out and picked up something small. With one hand cupped around it, he stumbled over to show me.

My stomach twisted.

In his hands was a young bird. Its head was covered with

tiny white feathers, but longer, darker feathers stuck out from its wings and back. One wing was held out at a funny angle. When it opened its mouth and squawked, we both jumped and yelped. He almost dropped it.

When it tried to jump out of his hands, the bird flopped on its side. It seemed to be injured and wasn't strong enough to escape. It was scary, revolting, and pitiful—a bundle of messy helplessness. I swallowed, and the saliva in my throat tasted sour.

"Come on, Ash. Leave it alone. It probably has bugs. Its mother will come back and take care of it." I thought it would probably die, but didn't want to upset him.

"No!" Ash pulled it closer to his chest. "No!"

In the woods behind us, voices shouted our names.

"Alright. Okay. It's fine. Rescuing that thing is a good idea. But we need help. Lead me back to camp."

Ash put his cheek against the bird's head. He mumbled a string of words. They didn't make sense, but it was the most talking I'd heard from him.

As we followed the dark trail towards camp, flashlights flickered in the distance. Tasha had alerted the counsellors and they were spread out, calling our names. I looked for Grif and didn't see him. Willa wasn't there either.

The counselors formed a circle around Ash and me, and escorted us out of the woods. When we reached camp property, JB and Kirra waited with the ATV, parked close to Tasha. Ash tried to hide behind me. Moe stood on the fringe, head down, shifting his feet.

"Thank God, you're both okay." JB's voice cracked. His fist was clenched to his chest, and I wondered again if he was having a heart attack.

Kirra checked us over to assess our condition. "Hmmm . . .

you both *seem* fine. What's up with Ash? What's in his hands?"

"Tell them." I stepped away so they could see.

Ash thrust his arms forward, cradling his discovery as if it was treasure. "Bird. Broken. Fix."

JB and Kirra exchanged glances. Something—a message I didn't understand—passed between them. "They need help." Kirra put her hand against JB's cheek. "You know what you have to do. I'll make the phone call."

JB opened his mouth to say something, then closed it. He turned to the counselors gathered around us. "Everything's fine here. Head back to the campfire. Moe, you gotta take over for a while. Explain what's happened, then teach them a pirate song. Make it fun. We won't be long."

Moe and the rest of the counselors drifted away towards the campfire until the five of us were left. Kirra waved goodbye and helped Tasha across the field.

JB jerked his head at Ash and me and pointed at the ATV. "Get in."

Whoa! There was *no way* I'd get inside that piece of junk and drive around at night! What if JB had a heart attack? What if Ash freaked out? What if the bird died? What if I was a wimp?

"Okay," I said.

Still holding the bird like it was made of fine china, Ash followed me into the back of the ATV. JB heaved himself in and started the ignition. The engine roared. He turned the headlights on and reversed. When he shifted into forward and stomped on the gas, we lurched and braced our legs.

As he drove across the field, my butt bounced so hard my teeth rattled. I hung onto to a side rail, so I wouldn't fall out. Ash locked his legs and pulled his arms in tight to protect the bird. When we got close to the waterfront, JB wheeled left and steered between two **KEEP OUT** signs. There was an overgrown road that I hadn't noticed earlier. He gunned the engine and my head jolted.

"W-where are we g-going?" I had to scream over the wind and machine noise, but my words were loud and clear. For the first time in months—I felt alive.

JB yelled, "To the Sanctuary."

A BROKEN BIRD

~~~~~~~

I was so scared, I almost barfed. JB's ATV roared along an old laneway—in the *pitch dark*. Each time he swerved to miss a pothole, we almost fell out. The trees were close to the path and their branches whipped against the ATV. Ash didn't move. He held the bird and crooned like he was its mother.

JB drove to a ramshackle little building deep in the Sanctuary. It was spooky, like something from a horror movie. When we pulled up, there was a light on inside, and the shadow of a figure peered out the window. JB told us to get out and bang on the door. I asked JB if he was coming with us, but he turned away.

"Naw. It's not a good idea for me to go in." He sounded strange.

Mad? Embarrassed? What was wrong with him?

81

"Why aren't you coming with us?" I tried not to sound as scared as I felt. I figured JB was the adult in charge, and it was time for him to show some responsibility and protect us.

He pulled out a handful of candy from his pocket and unwrapped a caramel before he answered. "Naw. You'll be okay—she doesn't bite little kids. Leave the bird with her, and I'll get turned around so we can leave quick."

He popped the caramel into his mouth and clamped his jaw shut.

Ash and I climbed out of the quad. Before we reached it, the shack door opened wide, and the inside light poured out onto a pathway. An ancient woman dressed in a man's plaid shirt and baggy pants held up by suspenders stood there, waiting. She was tiny, with a long braid of white hair over her shoulder. Despite the thick glasses she wore, she squinted, as if she couldn't see. Her face was wrinkled like an over-baked potato.

"Come right in." Her creaky voice made me shiver. "Kirra phoned and said you were coming."

I wanted to turn and run.

Ash had other ideas.

He came close and held out his hands to show her the bird. It lay on its side and didn't move. She wore gloves, and gripped his arm to steady herself while she leaned in. He didn't flinch.

"Broken," he said.

I took a fast glance over my shoulder to check if JB was still there. I was half-afraid he'd take off and leave us, like we were Hansel and Gretel in the witch's house.

She straightened and adjusted her glasses. "This is an infantile Great Horned Owl. It's about ten weeks old, but its wing is damaged. They live in these woods. It's definitely discombobulated."

She held out her gloved hands and Ash gently deposited the

bird.

"Thank you, dear." She turned and went inside.

I wanted to run for the quad, but Ash shuffled along behind her, so I had no choice.

We followed her into a room with an old couch, a chair with a broken arm, and a table covered with magazines and books. There were empty cages piled everywhere. Just like the ones Hansel and Gretel were locked in. It was a dump.

Hoarder, I thought.

She placed the bird into a shoebox filled with ripped up newspaper. She must have read my mind, because she said, "Despite the rumours about me, the cages aren't for children. They're for injured animals that need to be treated. I used to have lots of patients. Most were released to the wild. Unless they died."

Died. Ohmigod. What's going on? Things died in this house. My stomach lurched. I squeezed my fists and looked out the window for JB. He'd turned the ATV around and had the headlights pointed towards camp.

Get me outta here.

The old woman's glasses slipped down her nose, and she paused to push them up. "Long ago, when the sanctuary was open to the public, they called me the Owl Lady."

Hands stretched to his side, Ash circled the room. Mouth open, he took in the furniture, books, walls and cages. "Wow. Beautiful."

"What a dear, sweet lad. Is he related to you?"

Startled, I did a double blink. *What was she talking about?* Hands raised, I backed away towards the door. "I barely know him. He's got special needs. He got scared and took off during the campfire program. We found this bird in the woods."

"This was meant to be." The Owl Lady stroked Ash's arm,

then patted his shoulder. He stiffened but didn't move. "One last time. Okay, dears—JB doesn't come near me anymore. He wants to leave. Now head back to Rainbow Wings."

"Come back. See bird." Instead of sounding strained, Ash's face was soft and eager. He liked the old woman.

The feeling seemed mutual.

"Of course, dear. Come during the day and follow the road you drove in on. Nobody else, though. When you and your sister come back, I'll teach you how to help a broken bird."

"I'm not—"

She interrupted to prevent me from saying anything else.

"Broken? Yes—you are—he is too. We're all broken."

After JB drove us back to our cabins, he took off without a word of explanation. Before I fell asleep, I grabbed my journal and drew a map to the Owl Lady's house. Then I added the note: '*The drive back from the Sanctuary was . . . what? I was* _discombobulated_— *whatever that is!*'

ROUTINES

~~~~~~~~~

The days were busy and passed quickly, and before long, my life had developed a predictable pattern. My day started with breakfast in the cafeteria with the Bobcat LITs, then we separated for activities. The dance routines got more complicated as Willa added spins, jumps, twists and hand jives. One morning, she had us try on tap shoes. It was hilarious.

I'd danced in talent contests but had never tried to tap. We learned a basic ball heel shuffle. Lift, ball dig—repeat. Ball dig, heel drop—repeat. Brush forward, brush back—repeat. When I got used to it, it was a blast. *Bang bang bang.* When we danced together, it sounded like a hailstorm.

The yoga classes helped me relax and my muscles loosened and stretched. Who knew I could be a pretzel? The poses had names like Mountain, Tree, Downward Dog, Halfmoon—I learned a new language. Tasha's Arts and Crafts classes got frantic as she worked our sketches into set designs and props for the SHIVERS! musical. A tech group built the sets and we painted, and painted, and painted the pieces.

Whenever Grif had a break in his schedule, we met at the beach. After I learned to relax and float, it got easier. He helped me learn to swim. Grif was kind and funny. And we were never alone. The waterfront was a popular place. In the afternoons, the younger campers came for lessons. Even Ash got over his fear of the water.

He was still loud, and anywhere he went, everybody knew Ash was there. Moe didn't use the restraint anymore, but stayed close to prepare Ash for anything that might upset him. Occasionally, Ash had a panic attack and the activity stopped until Moe helped him relax.

Ash didn't like to wear a life jacket, and would chirp and argue about wearing it. Tasha asked Moe about it one morning, and he said it probably reminded Ash of the harness.

It's a 'trigger', Moe said. "Something that agitates him."

Tasha helped Ash paint a pirate treasure map on the back of a lifejacket, using waterproof paint. After a day of refusing to use it, he put the jacket on. When Moe invented raps and rhymes, Ash loved it. He'd memorize and repeat Moe's silly words until they were smooth. Afterwards, he'd yell, "HA!" or "ARRRRR!"

One day, the heat was brutal. By noon, we were all sweating. Tasha and I left the cabin together so she could set up for the arts and crafts class. Overhead, the sky was filled with a mass of grey clouds. We looked across the lake, and saw a storm in the distance. The wind blew hard, and on the horizon, there was rain falling on the mainland.

"It's headed our way. Let's get inside before we get poured on." Tasha pointed at the sky and spun around.

"Run!"

The words were just out of her mouth when the storm hit.

Everybody turned and charged for the main building. When we got there, I helped Tasha work her way through the crowd at the door. JB and Moe were already inside the cafeteria and after everyone squashed in, they did an impromptu rain dance.

It was fun, especially because coloured dye dripped from our soaked t-shirts and ran down our bare arms. I wasn't the only person with blue skin anymore.

Ten minutes later it was over. The sky cleared, and the sun came out.

As soon as the door opened, we all rushed out to the field. The ground was soaked and the pathways were full of puddles.

"Look at that!" someone shouted.

We stopped and stared at the sky. The world's biggest, brightest rainbow arched over the lake and landed in the water.

A boy from the Bear cabin pointed and yelled, "There's two!"

He was right. A second, fainter arc glowed in the distance.

I thought about the weird question JB had asked me on the first day.

It was noisy because everyone was excited and talking. Even though I knew it was pointless, I listened for the sound of a rainbow. Above the chatter, I heard two people laugh. It was Grif, flirting with Willa.

He's being friendly. He's always like that. It doesn't mean anything.

"Want to go for a walk tonight after supper?" I overhead him say.

"Sure." Willa fluttered her long eyelashes.

I watched her twist her long hair into a knot on the back of her head. My stomach made a knot, too.

About a week after we left the baby owl with the old lady, JB told us to spend the afternoon in our cabins, and called the senior counselors to a special meeting. The Bobcat girls and the junior counselors were supposed to organize indoor activities and supervise the campers.

Inside Tasha's private bedroom, I helped her put on a tight pair of shoes. I knelt at her feet, slipped a finger between her heel and the shoe, and eased her foot in. When I glanced at her face, her expression was tight and her brows were furrowed.

"Did that hurt?"

She shook her head, but I could see she was upset.

I straightened up and asked, "What's going on?"

She shrugged and gestured for me to lean in, so she could whisper.

"I dunno, Raven. Something's wrong. All this afternoon's activities are cancelled. It's so strange. We *never* get called to meetings in the middle of the day."

When she was almost ready to leave, she told the LITs to organize a quiet indoor afternoon for the younger girls. "I want you to hang out in different cabins. The guys have got supervisors for their side. Look in the cupboards. There are board games, cards, and art supplies. Make sure the campers stay inside their cabins. Nobody goes near the waterfront or leaves the property. Nobody."

Spex and Sticks stacked games and cards at the centre table. Rip lay in her bunk and closed her eyes.

"Gimme a minute to relax, and then I'll get some craft stuff

88

out," she grumbled.

Rapunzel paused at the mirror, comb in her hand. "If we had an internet connection, we could check our social media and talk to our friends. I've got *no idea* what's happening."

"You can call your parents tomorrow," said Tasha. She opened the front door and went down the ramp. From the bottom she yelled, "Make sure everyone stays out of trouble while I'm gone. I'm serious!"

It was hot and boring inside the cabin. The LITs made their plans to supervise and entertain other cabins. I felt isolated, because I wasn't part of the group and had no responsibilities. After they left, I took out my journal and wrote for a while. My eyelids felt heavy, and I had trouble staying awake.

"I'm going for a walk," I said to the empty cabin. Maybe the blood-swollen mosquito that bounced against the window heard me.

It was hazy and humid. The heavy thunderhead clouds in the sky meant another summer storm was coming. No one was around, so I wandered down towards the waterfront. When I was almost there, I saw Moe standing with Ash by the entrance to the old road leading to the Sanctuary. Ash was using a stick to draw in the dirt.

When he saw me, Moe's face brightened.

"Perfect timing, Raven! I need to attend the counselor's meeting. But I don't want to leave my buddy alone here. You're almost old enough to be a leader here, and he likes you. Can you stay, and hang out with Ash while I'm gone?"

Ash put down the stick and smiled at me.

There wasn't much choice; I wasn't supposed to be outside, but now I had a legitimate excuse. I liked Moe. When he rapped and sang at campfires, it was a blast. And I was getting used to Ash.

"Sure."

"Just don't go near the waterfront and don't do anything

stupid." Moe gave Ash a high-five, turned and sprinted for the office building.

"Now what?" I stretched my arms and lifted my hands to the sky. Ash laughed and pointed down the path.

"Owl lady. Find broken bird."

I was amazed ... *and* a little nervous. *That would be breaking the rules ... and what if we ran into a bear?* "I dunno—"

"Let's go!" Ash stuck his tongue out, turned and ran ahead on the old road. "Race—"

I had no choice but to run after him. "Ohmigod ... you *little* jerk! Wait for me!"

BLACKBEARD

~~~~~~~~

As we jogged along the Sanctuary lane, vicious flesh-eating deer flies swarmed around our heads. I'd learned from painful experience that if I got bit, it would feel like they'd grabbed a chunk of my flesh. Even though it always caused an ugly case of hat-head, I'd also learned to wear a hat. My mosquito bites itched, so I scratched a big, juicy one on my arm.

It made my skin tingle. Once, when she'd caught me scratching, Tasha'd said, "You need to get help to stop doing that. Those sores will get infected."

Who cares? Ms. Bossy wasn't around now to tell me what to do.

Ash ignored the bugs and trotted ahead. I ran hard to catch up, but wished I'd gone to the bathroom before I'd left Bobcat cabin. When I got closer, I heard him hum the pirate song the camp practiced each night. He'd added an annoying emphasis on the *Yo Ho* chorus.

Then he grabbed a long stick from the ground, and waved it around, pretending it was a sword. Every few minutes he'd take a pose, point it at an invisible enemy and yell, "Avast! Stand back you scurvy dog! ARRRRR!"

The trail to the Owl Lady's home went past a broken rail fence that surrounded a pond full of waterlilies. A grey wooden boardwalk led around the water, but the wood was broken in places, so we couldn't explore. At the top of a hill, we stopped and checked out the view.

In the distance, the area around the Owl Lady's shack was overgrown with weeds and saplings. Tall grass and late summer wildflowers filled in the surrounding fields. Cicadas buzzed, and grasshoppers leapt around our feet.

From our position, we had a view of the entire pond. In the middle, surrounded by the lily pads and flowers, there was a gigantic mound of branches. A dark shape swam nearby, making a v-shaped ripple on the water. Then it splashed and disappeared.

"Ash, that was a beaver!"

He pointed his sword at the heap of branches. "Lodge. Beaver house."

"You're right!" He stood still as I flicked a fly off his ball cap. "You're a smart guy. I didn't know *what* that pile of sticks was."

"ARRRRR!"

"ARRRRR!"

By the time we got close the Owl Lady's shack, I needed to pee so bad I was scared I'd wet my pants. I didn't want to earn a new label: 'Pee-girl.' There was no place to hide, and I didn't want Ash to watch. I estimated the distance to the old woman's place.

In daylight, it was obvious that her shack wouldn't last much longer. The exterior wood had faded to silvered grey. Thick green moss covered the tin roof. A sagging chicken wire fence, surrounded an old, overgrown vegetable garden where a scrawny red hen pecked.

An old barn stood behind her building, with holes in the roof and walls. Scattered around the property were run-down huts. Not far away, near a stand of maple trees, and surrounded by low bushes, leaned a red shed that looked like an out-house. Then I wondered if she even *had* an indoor toilet.

I wouldn't make it as far as her home.

I jiggled up and down and tried to figure out how to deal with my bursting bladder.

I was so desperate my teeth chattered.

"Wait for me here, Ash. I'll be right back."

I thought I was going to pee. Each step shook my bladder. As I pranced along towards the out-house, I undid my jeans and unzipped the fly. Holding my breath and clamping my teeth together, I yanked the door open and stepped inside.

When I closed the door, the space inside was as dark and disturbing as my worst nightmare. Staring me in the face was a big, black hole. With no toilet seat. The stink made me gag. I was afraid I'd fall in, but it was too late to be fussy. With my eyes shut, I crouched and did my business.

After a shudder and a deep breath, I opened my eyes and peered around. Cobwebs and spiders dangled from the ceiling and along the walls. Ugh. A tattered, yellow roll of toilet paper was stuck on a big rusty nail.

It got worse. Outside the door, I heard heavy breathing.

Footsteps crunched in the grass, as whatever it was walked around the back of the out-house. My skin felt like it was covered with little needled-footed bugs. Crawling up my arms.

It could be as simple as a raccoon. I could yell at that. Or ...
it could be a bear. Everyone had warned us. We'd been stupid to
walk alone in the woods!

I pulled up my pants and searched for a defence weapon.

An old ripped newspaper was stuck in a cubby on a side wall.
I lifted it out, shook off a spider, rolled it into a tube and slowly
pushed against the door. The door moaned. A long, drawn out
sound like something from a horror movie's soundtrack.

Something snapped behind the building.

The thing stalking me was hidden in the bushes. I could sense
its presence. Waiting. Breathing hard. I couldn't see it, but knew
it was big.

Ash! I froze. I'd abandoned him with no explanation. What
if he'd bolted into the words?

"Ash! Where are you?"

I heard the *ripppp* of a zipper. Ash stepped out from the bushes.
He'd been taking a leak.

"Here. Come *on* Raven, let's *go*!" Waving his hands, he jogged
away.

Whew! I felt so relieved, I almost laughed.

As we got nearer to the Owl Lady's shack, a flock of birds
chased each other. They swooped into the open spaces in the barn's
upper loft, where the old boards had fallen off. In the long grass,
large cages were scattered around or piled in messy heaps. The
cages were twisted and bent. Several had broken perches for birds.

The old driveway was lined with a row of large wire enclosures.
Faded signs dangled from posts outside them. *Great Horned Owl.
Hooded Merganser. Raccoons. Skunks. Fox kits. Black bear cub.* The
enclosures were all empty. Clumps of yellow grass sprouted in the
dirt floor and straggled in through the fence holes.

It looked unloved. Lonely. Sad. Deep inside me, I felt a

strange sensation. It was the feeling of being dumped, or worse—abandoned. I blinked and bit my lip. I didn't want to cry in front of Ash.

He marched to the house and banged on the door. "Owl Lady. Want bird."

Nothing happened. He banged a second time.

I felt uneasy, like we'd intruded into a sacred place. "Ash, she might not be home. Let's go back to camp before it gets late. It'll soon be time for supper. It's pizza night."

There was a prolonged creak, and the Owl Lady opened the door. In the bright sunlight, she appeared even older and more fragile than she'd seemed at night. She wore the same plaid shirt and baggy pants.

"It's the twins!" She smiled, and her face filled with wrinkles. A cloudy film dulled her blue eyes. "Come in, my darlings."

Ash sauntered right in. I rolled my eyes and followed him, even though it felt wrong. She was almost blind. And confused. My skin crawled. We *didn't* look alike. Once again, it felt like a scene in a horror movie.

Inside, it was dark, and my eyes needed time to adjust to the light. Something soft and furry rubbed around my ankles. Must be her cat, I thought. I glanced down and nearly fell over.

It was a skunk. In the cartoons, when people are scared, their hair stands straight up.

I think mine did.

"Isn't he sweet? Percy likes you. Don't worry, dear. He's been de-scented. He's a rescue. Someone found Percy laying on the road on the mainland and brought him to me. He'd been hit by a car. He'll never be safe in the woods, so he keeps me company."

Just as if it was a cat, Ash bent over and stroked the skunk. I gagged and thought I'd throw up. He crooned to it, "Don't worry,

Percy. Pirates don't eat skunks."

The Owl Lady smiled and patted the top of Ash's hat. He didn't flinch. She seemed harmless, but I couldn't relax. My senses were on high alert. As long as she didn't offer us anything to eat, we'd be safe, I thought. *Who knows what kind of food she has in the house?*

"You've come to see your owl friend. It's doing fine. Percy's shared his favourite treat with it. Come and sit down. I'll put the tea on."

"What's Percy's treat?" I asked.

"Mice."

That reinforced my decision not to eat anything!

We cleared a pile of newspapers off the furniture. Ash plunked into a rocking chair, and I sat on the ripped edge of her saggy couch. While the kettle boiled, the old lady limped around, and babbled about her animals and the old sanctuary.

"It was busy here once. People used to arrive by boat with injured animals, and I took *every one* of them. They say I had a magic touch."

She tottered into a back room and came out a moment later, carrying a large cardboard box with the young owl inside, and set it on the carpet.

"Your raptor friend is now considered a juvenile. Its adult feathers and markings are quite evident. The feather tufts at the top of the head are starting to show. Its wing is much stronger."

The bird looked bigger as it stood up, spread its wings and gently flapped them. Ash left the skunk alone, and peered into the box. He was mesmerized and made hooting noises back to the owl. When Ash had found it, the bird's head still had bits of fluffy down. Now, its head feathers were grey and buff, and its big round yellow eyes were like a Hallowe'en mask. Dark feathers sprouted under its black beak.

It had definitely developed and changed.

I sat beside Ash and studied the bird. "Cool! What are you going to call it?"

"Blackbeard. ARRRRR!"

"Figures!" He made me laugh. "Sure, that's a great name."

The old lady went into the kitchen, fussing and chatting as she clattered her dishes. While Ash cooed over Blackbeard, I checked out the room. Old newspaper stories and photographs about the sanctuary were taped to the walls. The images were faded, but it was easy to recognize her in many of them. One puzzled me, so I looked at it more closely.

In the photo, the Owl Lady stood in front of her shack, with an adult Great Horned Owl on her arm. Its head was swiveled to the side, but I recognized the pointed feather tufts sticking from the top of its head. The owl was tall and stiff, and gripped her leather glove with its talons. A young guy with a big gap-toothed grin stood beside her, his arm around her shoulder.

Jelly Bean!

The caption underneath said: *Today, Faena Bean, better known as the Owl Lady, and her son Jim, were honoured by Town Council for their rehabilitation work on Rainbow Island. Jim and his rock band, 'The Loonatics' leave next week for a six-month tour of Europe and Asia.*

The Owl Lady's hands trembled as she tottered into the room, balancing a tray. The flowered teapot, chipped mugs and a little plate of cookies rattled. When she got to the middle of the room, the tray tipped, and everything slid. I held my breath. She lowered the tray safely to her coffee table, and I exhaled.

"Dears, would you like some tea?"

Ash was fascinated with the owl and ignored her.

"When Blackbeard fly?"

His sentences were becoming longer and easier to understand.

"Soon, dear." The Owl Lady rocked back and forth on the edge of her chair. "It's been so long since I've had company. My son doesn't come here anymore. I'm all alone."

I remembered that JB wouldn't get out of the ATV when we first arrived. Something bad must have happened between them. I tried to get her to open up.

"Is your son a musician?"

"He was. And good at it, too. Until he got too important, and did some bad things. Then he stopped coming here."

She stared at the ceiling like she was watching a dust mote and hummed. The owl flapped its wings, lifted out of the box and landed on the floor. Ash tried to touch its head and it snapped at him. He jerked his hand back and his face twisted.

I don't know what she could see, but the Owl Lady sensed what was happening.

"Your brother shouldn't touch it, dear. It's a wild thing. It will soon fly and return to the woods. If it isn't imprinted on a human, it'll be safer."

Ash understood. His expression softened. He stayed still and didn't try to get near it again. Instead, he hummed the camp's ridiculous pirate song. For some reason, it was a good choice. No, actually, it was the magic touch. It charmed the owl *and* the Owl Lady.

"The darling child's a singer." She pointed a shaky finger at me. "Dear, would you bring Betsie to me? It's hard for me to bend over and get her from that corner."

A guitar leaned against a corner of the room, almost hidden by a tattered chair, and a pile of wood for her stove. Beside it was a set of hand drums and percussion instruments, plus music books covered with dust, cobwebs, and mouse poop.

I climbed over the piles of newspapers and furniture, retrieved the guitar and placed it in her lap.

The Owl Lady tilted her head and studied us as if remembering old times. Then, she picked at the strings, tightening and strumming until the guitar was almost in tune. In my old life, I often listened to the band tune before the show performances, but this setting was totally bizarre. What was she going to do next?

I had no idea.

She strummed and sang, "La, la la." The owl hopped around the room. As she played, it seemed to get stronger.

"Yes." Her face brightened. "I've got the perfect song for the three of you. It's an old one that I taught to my son. Written by a cute gentleman who called himself a Beatle. I always thought that was a clever name—combining music and the insect kingdom. He was my favourite. Paul McCartney. This is a special song. It used to help my injured animals feel loved. It's called, *Blackbird.*"

Her voice was weak and scratchy. She picked out a chord, then played a tune about a broken-winged blackbird that sang at night. Her voice wavered as the lyrics urged the bird to learn to fly.

I recognized the music, but had never listened to the words before. Ash tapped his feet to the rhythm. The chorus repeated, and she nodded at me to join in.

Why'd she pick that song? Did she know what would happen?

As she sang, my skin flushed, and heat spread through my body. I felt sweaty and dizzy. The room began to spin. My mind detached, and traveled back in time. It was like I'd grown wings and flown to that place I'd tried so hard to forget.

My past.

Six months before coming to camp, I was a finalist in the TripleT contest. But I didn't win. Instead, I became a disaster.

Afterwards, my therapist, Dr. Hill helped me understand that I'd been a pleaser—always done whatever people asked, so they'd like me. It didn't work. I had no friends. No one to talk to, even if I *could* talk.

Even before my second hospitalization, I'd been diagnosed with clinical depression. I'd hidden in my bedroom, lurked online, and searched the deepest, darkest corners, fighting the trolls.

During that time, my father cheated on my mother. My mother, the former pop-star, who'd made *my* success *her* career obsession. I never wanted to sing again. Then, I took 'the cure' and everything got worse.

As quickly as they'd come, the bad memories vanished. I came back to the present moment, and tried to sing the chorus along with the old lady. But the lump in my throat was so big, I couldn't manage a word. I whispered the last line. It was about waiting for the right moment. And then freedom.

Ash tapped the rhythm, and when the Owl Lady put the guitar aside, he clapped and put his fingers in his mouth and whistled. It scared Blackbeard. The little owl flapped its wings and briefly lifted off the ground. It landed with a thud and scurried under a chair.

"Your friend's getting better. There might be a mouse under there that Percy missed." The Owl Lady handed me the guitar to put back. "Would you like another cup of tea?"

We hadn't touched the first pot she made, but I didn't want to point that out. I carried the tray into her cramped kitchen and poured everything down the sink. When I opened the fridge to put the milk away, except for a cartoon of eggs and a loaf of bread, it was empty. I wiped my hands on a dish towel and said, "Ash, let's go back to camp. It's time for supper. It's your favourite. Pizza and corn on-the-cob."

The Old Lady pushed herself to stand and leaned on her chair. Her lips had a bluish tinge to them, and she wobbled. I wondered if she wanted to tell us something.

"We have to leave, but are you okay?" I said. "Do you need any help? Can we get someone for you?"

She shook her head. "Come back again. Your young friend will fly away soon."

It was late, so Ash and I ran back to Rainbow Wings.

We heard Tasha's and Moe's voices in the distance before we were out of the sanctuary property. They were waiting for us on the edge of the property. Moe shifted his balance back and forth, cupped his hands and shouted our names.

"Awesome!" Ash ran towards them and gave Moe a knuckle-bump. Then he scooped handfuls of acorns and pinecones from the ground, shoved them in his pocket and grabbed a long stick from the side of the path.

Moe's eyes widened and his jaw dropped. "What happened to him? He's so happy he's busting open!"

"We checked on the bird. It's doing better. It's almost ready to go free."

While the four of us headed back to camp, I absent-mindedly scratched my mosquito bites. Tasha gave me a look, and I stopped.

"I don't get it," I said. "The Owl Lady is JB's mother. But that house is in terrible shape. Why are the *No Trespassing* signs stuck all over the place? JB's always telling *us* about peace and love. She shouldn't be alone. So why doesn't he help her?"

Tasha and Moe exchanged glances.

"It's a long story," she said. "Tonight, you've got a private call with your parents. But you need to know something, first."

An unspoken message passed between them, and they both seemed uptight.

Moe helped Tasha across the bumpy field and said to Ash, "How fast can you run to the cafeteria? Can you beat my record?"

The challenge worked. Pretending he was charging into battle, Ash raced ahead waving the stick at imaginary enemies. Once he was out of earshot, Tasha told me about the special meeting they'd had with JB.

"He was shaking. I've never seen him like that. Almost in tears."

"Someone's betrayed him," said Moe.

"I don't get it. What happened?" I said.

"He heard from some angry parents. They want to take their kids out of Rainbow Wings. And they want their money back."

Then Moe chimed in.

"Someone's leaked bad press—fake news—to social media. To newspapers. And it's spreading out of control. Saying the kids regularly run away and get lost in the woods. That kids can't swim, but they pass the tests anyway. The supervision isn't careful. Our buildings aren't safe and won't pass health inspections."

"That's *not* true. Does he know who's doing this? Or why?"

"All summer, JB's been worried about the camp's finances. It's always tight because he keeps the camp fees low, despite all the staff. This summer's been expensive."

Tasha was out of breath, and Moe took over.

"When Ravi got hurt on the Obstacle Course, the media coverage was terrible. And of course, the press *didn't* share how JB paid for Ravi's helicopter and extra medical expenses out of his own pocket. Covered his salary for the rest of summer *and* his university tuition. It cost JB a fortune." Moe lowered his voice. "It was Ravi's own stupid fault. He snuck out on the obstacle course one night, without any safety gear. He wasn't found until morning. Even then, they smelled alcohol on his breath."

Tasha added, "In the hospital, Ravi told us it was a dare. Said someone else was with him—but none of us were there." She swatted a mosquito on her arm, then continued. "Just before this session started, JB paid extra to hire Grif. They had to give him a bonus and didn't assign him any special needs campers."

Tasha and Moe paused and locked gazes.

What were they thinking?

Moe resumed helping Tasha over a bumpy stretch and we saw Ash join the lineup for supper. Ash pretended to be a pirate, sword fighting with his stick. Then he stepped out of line and started to juggle something too small to see.

"Tonight, JB's going to talk about it at the campfire. He asked the counselors to check the cabins to see if someone's hiding a phone. Whoever it is, when he finds out ... JB will send them home. Fired." Tasha banged her fist on her lap.

We'd reached the door of the cafeteria. The Bobcat, Bear and Moose Cabin campers already waited in the lineup and Ash stood at the back. He jiggled and rubbed his hands together.

"Pizza! Corn! Ash hungry!"

Moe grinned. "You know, Ash is incredible. At first, I didn't believe his mom about his potential. He's come a long way in a short time."

I watched Ash juggle the six pine cones that he'd found. He did a fast spin around, and didn't drop any.

"I was in the office when he registered and overheard his mom talking about a trauma. There was something about his dad." I tapped Moe's arm. "Do you know what happened?"

"Some of it." He rubbed his forehead with the back of his

hand. He tipped his head to signal me to move out of the lineup, and lowered his voice. "You're amazing with Ash and he likes you. I'll tell you, but it's *completely* confidential. Each senior counselor gets a private briefing before their campers arrive. We take special training to help understand the kids who need extra support. Keep this to yourself."

Oh no. Another secret.

I glanced over at the lineup. The kids were restless, and the Bear cabin boys were play-fighting with their ball caps. Tasha moved into the line behind Ash; I had a feeling she knew what Moe would say.

"No question—Ash has *always* been different, but he's smart and like other kids in many ways. Is he on the spectrum?" Moe shrugged. "I'm not a doctor. He's a very complex person. There's no blueprint in the human brain that we can read to explain behaviour. Everyone is unique. There's always room for surprises— and for change. Ash is better at stuff that takes concentration ... like juggling."

Moe lowered his voice. "When Ash was ten-years old, his father said he couldn't deal with it anymore. There was a big fight. His father walked out, and never came back. Ash was traumatized."

Wow. My knees wobbled, and I swayed. Moe grabbed me by the elbow.

"You okay? Ash is doin' *great* here. His mom said he'll get more support at a new school in September. And she's got a new boyfriend. It's a good thing for them both. He's a teacher and understands Ash."

I walked in a tight circle until I got dizzy and had to sit on a bench. Moe sat beside me and we watched the cafeteria door open, and everyone file inside. I clasped my hands together and leaned forward.

"I came here ahead of time, with Ash and the other kids with special needs."

Moe leaned forward, elbows on his knees. He nodded. "Right."

"That means Tasha—got filled in on my background."

He nodded again.

My stomach twisted. Jaw clenched tight, I walked away from him.

"Hey, where you going?" Moe tried to follow me, but I brushed him away.

"I'm not hungry. I have a headache. I want to lie down. Tell Tasha I'll talk to her after supper."

Alone in the cabin, I lay on my bunk and worried.

What am I going to say to Tasha tonight? She knows everything about me. All my secrets and lies.

It seemed a long time since I'd arrived at Rainbow Wings. And at first, I hadn't planned on staying. Then things got better. But now, I wanted to run away. Fast. If only I had my phone, I could call a cab . . . no, a helicopter . . . the harbour police...to take me away!

So many things were confusing. My mind swirled. I took out my journal and wrote: *Who can I trust?*

There were a lot of secrets at camp. Too many for me to handle. I felt the black pit that had sucked me down in the past coming back. It would make me do things. Bad things. That's what I had tried to explain to Dr. Hill in my therapy sessions.

I wanted to hurt myself.

But for the first time, I didn't.

DARKNESS

~~~~~~~~~~

After supper, when Tasha and the LITs arrived, I was lying face down on my bunk. Tasha had a brought me a slice of Hawaiian pizza and a pile of salt-and-vinegar potato chips. The other girls ignored me, so I sat alone and picked at the food, even though I love pineapple on pizza. When I finished eating, she called us together for a cabin huddle.

"Guys—JB's worried. He won't talk about it at campfire tonight because the program's already set. Everyone's excited about the dance, and he doesn't want to ruin that. And some of you have the weekly call-home session tonight."

She put her hands together, closed her eyes and took a deep breath.

"Here's the thing … this is an awesome camp! We work together to make it a good place. Once in a while, shit happens, and we fix it and move on. But somebody's leaked terrible stories—blatant lies—to the media. Somebody has a phone and wants to destroy the camp."

She stopped, and the girls reacted in a jumble of sound.

"That sucks—"

"—fake news!"

"That's terrible!"

"What creep would do that?"

"I love this camp!"

"When I talk to my parents, I'll tell them the truth."

Tasha waited until it was calm. "We're a team here. If you know who has a phone or who's spreading lies, tell me! JB's worried the bad press will ruin everything. Parents might pull their kids out and never come back. He's afraid he's going to lose Camp Rainbow Wings."

She crossed her arms and rocked a moment, thinking. "And there's another thing. The developer who's building on the mainland wants to put a waterpark here. He's put pressure on JB to force the camp out and take over."

Tasha looked around the room, then directly at me. She didn't say anything, but somehow, I felt quilty—even though I hadn't done anything wrong! I put my head down and cleared away the leftover food and dishes.

"It's time to get ready for the campfire and dance. Raven, I'll go with you to the office, so you can talk to your parents."

"Sure. As soon as I get dressed for the dance, we can leave."

"On the way over, we can have a chat." Tasha touched my arm. "It's time."

PARTY TIME

~~~~~~~~

It was chaos in our cabin as six teenage girls got dressed for the dance. Suitcases were snapped open on the bunks, stuff pulled out, outfits tried on, then taken off. and new ones put on. Rapunzel found a feather boa, wrapped it around her neck and struck a pose. Squeak and Spex got into an argument over a pair of shoes. Sticks got upset when Rip pointed out how even the smallest top was too big on her.

The girl drama reminded me of being in the dressing room, backstage with the other TripleT contestants. I'd never cared about them, to be honest, they were—in a way—the enemy. Why befriend the competition? What was the point? At the end of each episode somebody was kicked off the show. Why be friends with someone who wanted you to mess up and lose?

I didn't need friends anyway; I had my parents.

Until that night at camp, no one had worn makeup, but Tasha said it was okay for the dance.

"Go for it! Have fun. Add colour or sparkles. I brought over some supplies from my classes that you can use."

In the middle of our cabin table, she placed false eyelashes, hair extensions and wigs. She'd raided the costume and props department for fake jewelry, shoes and hats.

I helped Squeak and Spex find shoes to match their outfits and did Stix's make-up. When Rapunzel dropped her bobby pins on the floor, Rip and I collected them and helped fix her hair.

It was like being in my dressing room a year ago but sharing it with girls who weren't my enemies. They were nervous, excited. Just like I'd felt in the past. I adjusted a cute maroon beret with a long green feather that curled under my chin.

"Will all the other campers dress up like this?" I dabbed concealer on a forehead zit.

"Only this cabin. The LITs have to help tonight, and this makes them stand out. We need to make sure everyone's having fun." Tasha went around the room, peeked into open suitcases, oohing and ahhhing at the other girls' outfits. She wore faded jeans, a sequined tank top and a fluffy pink feather boa. She'd put on extra makeup and one of the tri-cornered hats from the SHIVERS! costumes. A painting of a tropical island complete with palm trees and parrots was taped to the back of her chair.

The way she gushed over the girls' stuff made me suspicious.

I figured she was scouting to see if there was a phone hidden in someone's bag.

Then I felt guilty.

I knew who had a phone.

But it was legit. Grif was a counselor. What he was doing was a surprise for JB. He didn't want to ruin the camp.

Two bunks over, Sticks lay on her bed, tugging on a pair of tight jeans.

"Raven, are you hooking up with Grif at the dance? You're spending a lot of time at the waterfront. I don't blame you—he's hot." She groaned, and I heard a zip.

My face burned. Before I could reply, Tasha shot me a look and butted in. "Of course not. Counselors aren't allowed to date campers. Raven's training for her school swim team. That's why she's at the beach every day."

"But we're not regular campers, are we?" Rapunzel was in front of a mirror with a curling iron. "We're the Leaders-in-training. Those rules don't apply to us."

Tasha heaved a sigh. "The two most important rules here are for *everyone*. Kindness and honesty. We live by those rules. The counselors are older than the campers, and in a power position. When summer ends, we'll go back to our regular lives. It'd be wrong for a counselor to have a relationship with someone younger and vulnerable ... and then dump them at the end of camp."

In the middle of her monologue, she stopped and glared at us.

"It's happened before, and it was a *stinking mess*. Building healthy relationships is at the heart of Rainbow Wings. No one should leave here with a broken heart—especially by a counselor."

It was a long lecture, and Drill-Sergeant Tasha's words almost ruined the fun of preparing for the dance. The LITs went silent and put away their suitcases.

Tasha headed for the exit door. "Raven, let's go to the office and call your parents."

My stomach churned as I grabbed my purse and hurried after her.

TASHA'S RULES

It was easy to see that Tasha was upset with me. She travelled so fast along the path to the admin building that I had to jog to stay with her. Her breath came in little puffs. When we were out of the LITs' listening range, she pulled over to a bench and pointed at me to sit.

"Your conference call isn't scheduled for a few minutes. Your parents will meet with you privately, then JB will come on and you'll all talk about your progress. Is there anything you want to talk about beforehand?" She sounded tense.

I sat still for a moment. A red squirrel climbed a tree beside me and chattered as if it also had the right to lecture me.

"Kindness and honesty," I said. "Those are the camp rules

that we should live by." I tried to eliminate the sarcasm. I wasn't convinced, but she was a believer and that's what she wanted to hear.

"That's what it all boils down to." Tasha leaned back so she had a view of the sky. The sun had dropped lower on the horizon and the sky was streaked with elongated pink and purple clouds. "Raven, you haven't been honest with me—"

"They briefed you about me before I arrived. Right?"

She nodded.

"You know I don't have brothers and sisters ... and I'm not here on a scholarship."

She nodded again.

"You know my background ... my singing career ... how it ended and why I'm here."

Tasha said nothing. Her round brown eyes stared into mine. It was like she could see inside my head. We stayed like that—not talking—just sitting. Maybe I was in shock.

I thought about the dance and wondered if I'd get a chance to be with Grif.

Briefly, I wondered if Tasha felt bad about not being able to dance.

"It's your turn to be honest, Tasha. Why am I in a cabin with the LITs? I'm not planning to be a counselor."

"JB made an exception when he placed you in Bobcat cabin. The LITs are the oldest campers here. Because of your age, he thought you'd fit in, and it'd be the best placement for you. Especially considering your past and needs. The other LITs signed up months ago. They're nice people. One dropped out unexpectedly, so it made room for you."

"Did he ask you to work with me?"

"Yes, and I'm trying my best, Raven, but not having a lot of success. I'm going to be honest. Everybody here tries to get along—

and at least make friends with their cabin mates. You don't make much effort. The only person you seem interested in—besides yourself—is Grif."

"That's none of your business." I backed away from her. "I don't need your opinions or any help with my life."

Tasha turned bright red. "I understand—but I'm worried about you, and want to help. And Grif . . . well, he wasn't trained like the rest of us . . . he's so new, I haven't figured him out. There's something about him . . ."

She looked away for a moment, then took my hand. "Raven, I care about you. Promise me you'll give the others a chance—and please, please, be careful."

I pulled my hand away and glared at her. She gave me some time to stew, then poked me with her elbow.

"We better go. You're first in the line-up and other kids are waiting. Let's head to the office.

PARENTS

~~~~~~~~~~

When we arrived at the office reception, a few campers were already there, waiting for their turn. I recognized the ones who'd come on the ferry with me on the first day. Helmet and Big-boy seemed bored. They both smiled at me when I came in. After camp started, I hadn't had much to do with them. The other kids in the room were younger.

Ash was there, with Moe beside him.

When I went to her desk, Kirra glanced away from the computer and pushed her glasses back up her nose. "Raven! You're late. I was worried. You're supposed to arrive fifteen minutes before your call. You're the first person on tonight's schedule. The others will get their turns after you. Let's go."

She gestured at me to follow her to a small room at the back of the building. Sanjay, an adult staff member who lived on the property, was setting up for the video conference. The room was full of his recording and photographic equipment.

Kirra waved to him, then turned to me.

"Your parents talked to JB last night—so they have a sense of how you're doing. Sanjay will get you started, then step out. You'll have complete privacy."

Kirra flipped through some paper, and studied the schedule.

"Sorry, Raven. Because you're late, you'll have a short conversation. When you're finished, come back to the waiting area. After your call, Ash is next."

After she left, Sanjay helped me get organized at a desk in front of a large monitor.

When the call started, he stepped back. "Everything is ready. I'll wait in the Infirmary. If you have trouble, come out and get me." He clicked a remote. "You're on your own now ... good luck!"

The monitor flickered and glared with white light. Then it turned an ugly pea-soup green and broke into a set of squares filled with multi-coloured boxes. The fuzzy images cleared and there sat my parents, in separate boxes, like we were in cages. I almost burst out laughing, because it seemed so appropriate. I couldn't ever remember an occasion when Suzi and Jon sat together, face-to-face and listened to me. Suzi was first to speak.

"Hi, honey! How's camp going?"

Before I could answer, Jon's voice broke in overtop. "How's it going?"

The set-up felt uncomfortable and artificial. Occasionally, the internet connected faltered, and their faces froze, so it was hard to tell if they were listening. I was in a bad mood because of the earlier conversation with Tasha.

115

"It sucks."

They both blinked and sat up straight. We all stared at the monitors and no one spoke. My bites itched, but I forced myself not to scratch. It was the first screen I'd seen in a week. I'd never been offline that long in my life.

"What's wrong, sweetheart?" Suzi's tone seemed more angry than worried. "Why aren't you having a good time?"

"Because you forced this on me!" I snapped at her and shook my head. "What did you expect? A magical transformation and I'd become your perfect little robot singer again?"

She winced and leaned away from the camera. Then she stood and my view was of her headless torso. Dressed in an old t-shirt and hoodie, instead of her usual designer clothes.

Jon ignored her and talked in the fake happy voice he'd used before I left for camp. "Hi, sweetheart! Nice to see you. Made any new friends? Enjoying the activities?"

"I already told you. This place *sucks*."

My mother sat down, and her face came back into view. Maybe it was the lighting, but she appeared tired. There were more lines on her face than I'd ever noticed before. Her hair was flat and she wasn't wearing lipstick. She seemed ordinary instead of glamourous.

I felt a tinge of guilt for being a grouch. "What's happening at home? Have you found a new house for us?"

"Not yet. But I've sold the Beamer—"

"What? My BMW!" That was a shock. She loved that car; we both did. Early on in my career, we'd agreed that some of the money that I'd earned singing at concerts and competitions, would go towards buying us a great car. Even though I was too young to drive, I felt like I owned it. Especially because I'd soon be old enough.

"Why?"

"I was offered a great price. I bought a little car that'll be perfect for us. It's red, with a black interior. In good shape and a reasonable price. I had money left over."

"Wha—?" I was repeating myself, but—couldn't she slow things down? Try to put our life back together? *Something*?

Jon had more surprises. "Suzi and I've agreed to put the house up for sale, and there's lots of interest. It'll sell soon. I've bought a condo in town close to work. I can't wait to show it to you!"

It was too much. They'd moved too fast. Had they forgotten about me?

I pushed the LEAVE MEETING button, and walked out.

RED LIPSTICK AND DIAMONDS

~~~~~~

I walked past Sanjay, who was reading a newspaper on the Infirmary
nit stool. His eyes widened. "All finished?"

I walked past the kids waiting near Kirra's desk.

I glanced sideways at her. "Tell JB I'll talk to him later."

I kept walking. She opened her mouth to speak, but said
nothing.

Tasha sat by the door, leafing through a magazine. One look
at me, and she dropped the magazine on the table. I yanked the
door open, and ran down the ramp. I heard puffing, and knew she
was coming after me. In her hurry, she left the door open.

In the background, Ash yelled, "My turn!"

I ran back to Bobcat cabin as fast as I could, and Tasha didn't try to stop me. I flung the cabin door open and yanked my suitcase out from under my bunk. The other girls had already left for the dance.

Shirts, shorts, bathing suit, summer dresses, underwear ... then I found it. A skimpy, flesh coloured bra-top covered with sparkly diamonds and tiny pearls. Totally unsuitable for camp, and an outfit my mother hadn't bought or packed. She didn't even know about it.

At the last minute, on the morning I left home, I'd tucked it in. It was a leftover wardrobe piece from an old stage performance. The show's producer had given it to me. For good luck. He said he gave special clothing to all the pretty girls. The outfit had worked fine then for getting people's attention.

I used to be skinny, but I'd put on weight after the second hospital visit, and even more since coming to camp. My boobs were bigger, and the bra was tight. Sucking in my breath, I managed to hook the loosest clips on the straps. A quick glance in the mirror—it looked like I was naked from the waist up, but my breasts were covered with tiny jewels. I threw my jean jacket on over the bra-top and buttoned it. By the time Tasha entered the cabin, I was at the mirror adjusting my makeup.

She was out of breath. Her shoulders heaved from the effort of chasing me.

"Ahhh . . . everything okay?"

"Quit following me around, will you—"

"Sorry—you left in a big hurry—"

"Because I don't want to miss the dance." I put on red lipstick and pouted in the mirror.

Tasha gave me a long stare. "Sure. Ready to go now?"

"Sure. As ready as I'll ever be."

TRASHY TEEN PRINCESS

~~~~~~~~~

Even though I was on edge when I arrived, the dance-party started off great. The counselors and the camp band played cover songs. Some kids danced, some sang and waved props. The LITs partied with everyone.

No alcohol or drugs were allowed at camp, but something ran through my veins and made me high. I was wild with hunger and thirst.

Inside the cafeteria, there was a table loaded with junk food and drinks. Grif saw me cooling off on a bench and brought over a glass of fruit punch. It was cold and sweet with a funny taste I didn't recognize. He stayed with me as the band played another set.

Earlier in the day, three old dudes from JB's former band, 'The

Loonatics', had come over to the island on the ferry. After the camp band finished, they came on stage with JB and their instruments. I'd seen their photos in the office. The Loonatics were ancient, but awesome. The party took off. JB switched from bass guitar to drums. At the end of the set, they played an old song that everyone knew. We echoed the words and did hand motions.

I felt confident, singing with the crowd. Nobody noticed if I couldn't reach the high notes or sustain the volume. I played with the harmony and once in a while, it sounded okay to my ears.

I danced with lots of kids. Mostly with groups, including Bigboy and Helmet from the ferry, but I connected with Grif three times. When we were close, I undid my jean jacket, so he saw my boobs popping out the top of my sparkly bra-top.

Definitely, he noticed.

Leaning closer, he said, "Want to watch the stars with me afterwards?"

My skin felt hot. I knew I shouldn't. But then—why not? I swallowed hard.

"Okay."

"Meet me behind the cafeteria." He gave me a knuckle-bump.

The party finished at 9:30, and we were supposed to walk back to our cabins. JB told us to watch for a meteor shower on the way.

I told Tasha I needed fresh air and wanted to stay behind to look at the stars. She had a funny expression, like she was trying to read my mind.

"Okay. Don't be out late."

I was still mad at her, and it bugged me. *Jeezz ... does she think she's my mother?* While the other campers went to their cabins, I sat on a bench and looked around. I'd never been in a place so remote and dark. I stretched out on the bench with my jacket bunched under my head for a pillow to watch the meteor shower. It was incredible.

Like scattered diamonds, the stars sprawled across the black sky. It would have made a beautiful picture. A star streaked overhead, then disappeared. Not for the first time, I wished I had my phone.

When I was sure everyone had left, I snuck around to the back of the cafeteria. There was a glow, like from a phone, and I heard a quiet voice talking. Grif was hidden behind a tree and didn't see me.

As I got closer, I heard him say, "Sure. I'm getting the photos ready. It's all under control."

Photos? He was probably talking about the slide show he was making as a surprise for JB and Kirra on the last day. But who else knew? When I called his name, the light disappeared, and he stepped out.

Out on the lake, a loon wailed. A second one called back with a different waver. We both stood still and listened.

We were so close together we almost touched. My face burned. *Would he kiss me?*

He turned, and our eyes met. He leaned in closer and put a hand on my arm.

"It's beautiful here at night," I said.

"You're—"

We heard the motor of a boat pulling away from the waterfront and the sound of JB's ATV driving back across the field. The headlights were on and JB headed in our direction.

Grif stiffened, dropped his arms and stepped back. Without a word, he disappeared around the corner of the building. Before JB arrived, I put on my jacket and buttoned it.

JB stopped and called out to me. "Earth-child? Are you

watching the star show?"

"It's incredible."

"Aaahhhh, it's Raven. Time for you to head back to your cabin. You don't want Tasha to worry about you."

"Absolutely. I never want anyone to worry about me."

"And there's nothing here to worry about. Climb aboard and I'll give you a lift back."

It was after midnight; everyone was asleep, but I was still wide awake. A buzzing mosquito was driving me insane. To make my life worse, Rip's snoring was loud and clear. Once again, I wanted to put a pillow on her face. Just push it down while she squirmed and kicked until she stopped.

I pinched myself until it hurt. *Sorry sorry sorry; I don't mean it. Just please STOP the freaking SNORING!*

Near my bed, soft moonlight came in through the window. I got up and found a flashlight in the cupboard to give me enough light to write in my journal. I flipped through a few of the pages I'd worked on. When I first arrived at camp, I'd been scared, and had felt like an alien in a strange world. Then it became more interesting, and sorta fun.

But now, a lot of messed up stuff was going on.

I wrote a few lines about the dance, then closed the book and tossed it under my bunk.

LEADERS-IN-TRAINING

Early the next morning, the girls from Bobcat cabin sat around the breakfast table and dissected the dance. *Who wore what. Who danced together. Who's hot.* Rip had a fruit smoothie and rice cakes, Spex had scrambled eggs and bacon. Squeak and Stix had bowls of oatmeal and fresh fruit. Rapunzel had a blueberry waffle.

A camp rule was that each cabin table took turns to clear the dining area after the meals; it was Bobcat cabin's turn. While we waited for the rest of the tables to finish, Tasha said it was a good opportunity to discuss the SHIVERS! show.

"Time's flying! From this point on, all the camp activities shift into show rehearsals. Everybody's in their favourite group now. JB gave the senior counselors a show outline, and today's a tryout for the leads."

Instant drama. Looks were exchanged around the table. Plates were pushed away, and the girls crossed their arms and leaned back in their chairs. Rip spoke first.

"But we're all in the show, right?"

"Of course—it's an ensemble production. Each person here is in *at least* one feature number and can also be in the chorus. SHIVERS! is a comedy, but the pirate theme holds it together. Singing, dancing, juggling, uni-cycle, stage fighting ... all the stuff we've been working on fits together."

Tasha turned around to see if anyone else could hear her, and started again in a lower voice.

"JB's casting the lead pirates. There's a hero, a villain and some side-kicks. The script's funny, but it's got a few twists, and a dramatic rescue. The roles aren't gender or age driven. You can audition for any part."

"Even the counsellors? They can be in the play?" Spex poured herself a glass of water.

"It's so friggin' hot. I gotta keep hydrated."

And as they always did, Squeak and Stix copied her. The entire table drank water.

"Anyone can audition for any part," Tasha repeated. She swiveled and surveyed the emptying dining area. "Crap. Look at that."

We turned to see what she pointed at. Then we groaned, as a nearby table of campers walked away and left their table piled with dirty dishes and crumpled napkins.

"That's brutal. Those jerks could have at least picked up their own garbage. It's *not fair* that we have to do it. Tasha, who's their counselor? You should report them." Rip stood, hands on hips, and scowled.

Tasha moved away from the table and watched the boys

disappear out the café door, joking and slapping each other's shoulders. As if it was their special cabin cheer, they burped in unison. One yelled, "Cooties!" and threw another boy's ball cap in the air.

"That's the Bear cabin—Grif's campers. Strange. I don't see him. Haven't seen him all morning. He's not setting a good example, *or* supervising them." Her eyes narrowed.

"He'd be a great lead pirate," said Spex.

"If he had that role I'd try out for the opposite lead," said Rapunzel.

"Is there a love scene? Kissing?" asked Rip. "Raven could do that."

They caught each other's eyes and laughed until Tasha stopped them. "Whoa. No teasing. We're practicing being honest and kind."

Then she softened, "It's a comedy, remember? We respect each other, right? There's no romance in the play, or anywhere else at camp."

My nails dug into my fists. I wanted to scratch myself, but remembered how Dr. Hill had coached me to keep calm and avoid over-reacting to stress. I hadn't scratched for a while. I placed my knife and fork on the side of my plate.

"Everyone's gone. Let's clean this place and get back to our classes."

"Fine," said Squeaky. "But first, I gotta pee."

"Me too," echoed the others.

"Raven, I guess it's us to us to clean up." Tasha stacked the dishes at our table. "You can think about the auditions while we're working."

DISCOMBOBULATED

~~~~~~~~~

After Tasha and I finished clearing the tables, I felt discombobulated. It lasted all morning. That's how the Owl Lady had described the little owl. Like my limbs weren't connected to my body, or like my brain was filled with fog. It was a familiar feeling. After my breakdown, I'd tried to tell Dr. Hill about the scary sensation.

She'd made notes while I talked. After I'd finished the ramble about brain fog, black pits and doing dumb stuff, she'd nodded and put her pen down.

"Raven, this is a common experience when someone's overloaded with sensory input. The brain tries to organize input and make sense of it. It's similar to a computer searching for a solution. You've seen the little wheel spin on the screen. When there's too much information, a computer freezes. The same situation occurs when the brain's confused. It can't tell your body how to properly respond. There's a disconnect. That's when you make mistakes, make bad choices ... or act on impulses that you regret later."

Discombobulated. Somehow, the Owl Lady's word was a perfect fit for my problem.

Willa commented on my disconnectedness in dance class. She sounded concerned. "You're usually on top of things, Raven. You always get the steps the first time, and you're always on the beat. Today, you missed the cue several times. It's like your brain's not here. Are you okay?"

Later, in our yoga class, I couldn't relax. Willa had us lying on mats on the dock. We were supposed to concentrate on the sound of waves lapping against the dock. All I could focus on was the buzz of wake-boarders and water-skiers in the background. Rap music blared from the passing boats.

It didn't help my concentration that Grif was working on the beach nearby. He shouted at the campers as he taught them to paddle canoes and kayaks. Over all the shrieks and yells, I recognized Ash's voice.

He was obviously excited about something. He yelped, and there was a loud splash. I lifted my head to check on him.

Ash was standing up in Pegasus, the inflatable unicorn boat. His legs were braced and he shifted to keep his balance. He wore his hand-painted lime-green lifejacket with three black body straps. In his hands, he swung a kayak paddle, pretending that he was a pirate ship captain. He'd memorized a tune from the camp show and belted it out at the top of his voice.

With Ash's amazing ability to project sound—almost like he was a human megaphone—everyone heard him. Moe paddled in a canoe nearby, to encourage him.

The girl on a mat beside me lifted her head to watch. "That kid's come a long way in a short time. I remember when he first arrived, he was afraid of the water and he hardly spoke. Now, every day he says more stuff. Someone said he's memorized all the words to the SHIVERS! play."

A girl on the other side of me said, "He paddles to Treasure Island each day with Moe and works out on the obstacle course. I've heard that it's a cool place. We should talk Willa into taking us over there. There's a great beach where we could meditate."

Trying to relax, I lay back on my mat and closed my eyes. The sun felt warm and the waves splashed against the dock. As the noises faded, I put my arm over my eyes to block out the bright sunlight.

Someone talked to me from a great distance away. Willa. She sounded annoyed.

"Raven, wake up. You fell asleep. Again! Class is over and everyone's left for lunch."

I blinked, propped myself on an elbow and looked around. The waterfront was empty, except for Grif stacking the boats and paddles at the shore. The lifejackets were hung on the hooks at the beach hut.

"Whoa, sorry! Guess I was tired. Don't wait for me. Go ahead—give me a minute to wake up. My brain's foggy. I'll be there soon."

After she left, I studied the lake and the horizon. It was hazy and impossible to see the mainland. The Poseidon wasn't far away though; its shape was headed towards our dock. It had a set schedule and went back and forth with people, and food supplies. I hugged my knees and watched it come closer. The sun felt good on my back and I relaxed, watching the gulls swoop over the waves.

I must have zoned out again, because the Poseidon's horn's blast startled me, and it was tied to the main dock. Two of the full-time adult staff stood at the gangplank. They stepped onboard and unloaded boxes of groceries and other camp supplies onto the dock. An uptight-looking woman strode off the gangplank. Even from my distance, she seemed ready to explode.

A senior counselor waited on the dock beside a young kid in a camp t-shirt. A suitcase was beside the camper. The woman's shrill words carried across the water. I overheard her conversation with the counselor as clearly as if I stood beside her.

"I'm *outraged* by what I've heard! This is not a safe place for my son. We're furious about what's happened at this camp. Tell JB that I expect a full refund. When we get home ... if there's *anything* wrong with my boy ... JB will hear from my lawyers. I intend to sue."

The counselor's voice was soft, apologetic. "I'm sorry you feel that way, ma'am. There's been a misunderstanding. This is a wonderful place. If you want your son to leave, JB will refund your money. Let's go to the office and discuss this—"

The kid's high voice interrupted. "I don't *want* to go, Mom! I love camp!"

The mother was red-faced and rigid. She took her boy's hand, grabbed the suitcase and marched onto the ferry. The captain left the Poseidon and went with the counselor towards the main office.

An idea popped into my head.

When I first came to Rainbow Wings, I fell asleep each night making an escape plan. Sometimes I imagined that a helicopter would suddenly appear and lift me off. Sometimes a rich producer wanted me for another show and drove up in his yacht. During the night, I often dreamed I was back on stage, singing. It always ended in another disaster.

But nothing ever happened, and I was still stuck on Rainbow Island, covered with sunblock and inflamed mosquito bites.

It was simple. There *was* a way to ride the Poseidon back to the mainland. While everyone was distracted, I could sneak onboard. When we arrived at the other side, I'd ask someone to phone my parents. I'd complain and tell them the rumours. Then Suzi or Jon would come and rescue me.

It would all go back to the way it was before.

I grabbed my towel and mat, with my mother's words in my head. Suzi had an expression: *when an opportunity arises, go for it.*

But as I got closer to the ferry, the timing and situation didn't feel right.

In the shade of a clump of trees, there was some wooden furniture painted in rainbow colours. I sat on a blue chair hidden by overgrown bushes, and reconsidered. My escape plans never had me dressed in a purple bra and leggings and carrying a yoga mat. What if someone took a photo and shared it? I'd look like a fool. Again.

While I sat thinking the plan over, a grey-haired man dressed in khaki pants, a white hat and a golf shirt stepped off the ferry, glanced around, then removed his sunglasses. He stood brace-legged, hand shielding his eyes, and surveyed the waterfront. He seemed familiar. I wasn't sure but thought he might have been part of the group of contractors and businessmen Suzi and I noticed at the ferry terminal when she dropped me off.

Without noticing I was there, Grif ran past me, along the dock and shook the man's hand. For a second, I thought they were going to hug, but they both stiffened and stepped back.

Their backs were turned to me and the noise from a passing jet boat pulling skiers muffled their voices. I thought Grif said, "Everything's going great."

The man handed a package to Grif, turned around and boarded the ferry.

MORE SECRETS

~~~~~~~~~

When I touched back Grif's back, he jumped and whirled around. His face was tight, angry. Like he was caught in a trap. The package he'd been given was tucked under his arm. He hadn't noticed me watching.

He flinched. "What the f—?"

"It's just me. Can I walk with you?"

"I'm in a hurry. I slept in and JB chewed me out for missing breakfast with my cabin. Jerk."

"You got a package." That was a trick of Dr. Hill's. Instead of asking a question and getting a dodgy answer, state the obvious.

"So what?"

"That guy didn't stay long. Was that your dad?"

Grif's eye twitched. "Listen, don't mention this to anyone. We're not supposed to have contact with anybody—outside the weekly call. Mic's a business partner of my dad's. He dropped off some . . . junk food and new shorts for me. I spilled grease on another pair. On an embarrassing spot."

"It's our secret." I faked a laugh.

"So shut up about it. I know your secrets, too." He quickened his steps like he wanted to get away from me.

"Last night—" It was embarrassing. I didn't mean to sound so babyish. "I thought—"

Grif turned to face me. "Sorry, Raven, I didn't mean to sound so grouchy. I'm just stressed out trying to do a good job. Last night was great! Too bad that idiot JB interrupted us. We'll have to meet again soon."

"How about tonight, after the campfire ... same place?"

"Deal." He winked and smiled. "Wear the same outfit. Our little secret."

"Deal."

We walked to the cafeteria and went to our separate cabin tables. We were late, and by the time I grabbed my lunch and got to the table, the Bobcat girls had finished eating. As she pushed back from the table, Tasha gave me a funny look.

"Your face is flushed. Are you okay?"

"Fantastic."

"I've got to put out the craft supplies for this afternoon. Are you going swimming?"

"Yup. See you at supper!"

I ran back to the cabin, grabbed my bikini and towel off a clothesline strung between two trees, went inside and grabbed a pen. I wanted to tell the world that Grif was meeting me, but all I could tell was my journal.

CONFIDENCE AND TRUST

~~~~~~~~

The rest of the day was a blur. When I went to the waterfront, I was disappointed that Grif wasn't there. Another counsellor was in charge.

I practiced swimming back and forth between the camp docks, using a flutter board to strengthen my leg kicks. Then I imitated the arm movements that another counsellor was showing the beginning swimmers.

I missed the supportive feeling of Grif's hands under my back helping me float, but I didn't really need it. I relaxed, and floated. Waves from passing boats rolled in as I swam from one dock to the other, then back without touching bottom or stopping. At the edge of the dock, I spat out a mouthful of water and looked around.

Happy sounds came from the other end of the beach, where the little boats launched. "ARRRRR!" I recognized Ash's high-pitched scream.

Off-shore in a red canoe, Moe cheered. I waded out of the water to watch. Out in the lake, beyond the swimming area, Ash stood in the unicorn boat, maintaining his balance, while it bounced on the waves. He juggled a set of coloured balls the kids used for water polo.

The people on shore clapped and whistled.

"GO, ASH!" someone shouted.

A wave from a passing ski boat hit the side of the unicorn, and it tipped sideways. Ash almost lost his balance, lifted one leg like a stork and tilted. He nearly fell, but recovered. Then a larger wave hit the unicorn and dumped Ash into the water. The balls scattered around him. He was wearing his life jacket, but he panicked.

It was painful to watch.

Ash flailed his arms, screamed like he'd been attacked, and yelled something about crocodiles. Moe paddled over close to him, and kept the canoe steady a short distance away, out of Ash's reach. I couldn't hear what Moe told him, but it seemed to help.

Ash still flailed, but less hysterically. Then he stopped, and floated safely, his head bobbing above the water. The life jacket held him up. He slapped his arms on the surface and kicked his legs.

Moe leaned farther out of his canoe and held it steady. Ash grabbed hold of the closest edge.

"Careful. Reach all the way across!" Moe's instructions carried across the water. A wave hit Ash in the face and he choked and coughed. He pulled hard on the canoe, splashing and kicking, trying to climb inside.

The boat flipped over.

Moe dumped into the water and disappeared.

Willa was on lifeguard duty, watching from the tower. She blew a whistle and yelled at everyone to get out of the water. While the swimmers staggered onto the shore, she climbed down the steps and ran along the beach.

Out on the lake, there was a splash, and Moe's head rose above the surface of the water. His canoe was almost underwater, but the bottom was visible. It floated sluggishly, like a sick, red whale.

"Do you need help?" Willa waved at Moe.

Ash flailed his arms and legs like a windmill and screamed. Willa moved the shivering kids farther along the shore.

Moe didn't seem upset and shouted back, "We're okay! When he relaxes, I'll teach him to do a roll. Willa, tell them to sit still and watch. It's a good lesson."

"Can you touch bottom?"

"I sure can." He demonstrated with an arm raised above his head. "It's too deep for him, but he's fine. He's not gonna drown. He needs to trust me and listen."

Willa turned to the other kids and put her finger to her lips.

Moe murmured to Ash, but didn't touch him. Then Moe yelled, "ARRRRR!"

Ash responded, "ARRRRR!" He stopped flailing and began to tread water. He was calmer—alert and focused.

Moe signaled Ash to move to one side of the canoe. Moe swam around to the other side, pointed at Ash and yelled, "Now!"

Both heads disappeared.

"Did they drown?" A younger girl looked wide-eyed at Willa.

"They're dead!" Horrified whispers spread around the beach.

Willa shook her head. "Watch!"

She pointed at the canoe. As if by magic, the bottom rose high above the waves, and the water dumped out. Then the canoe flipped over, and crash-landed on the surface.

Ash and Moe's heads popped up, close together. They were talking, but their words were too quiet to hear. Ash stayed in place, and Moe swam to the other side of the boat.

"Now!"

In one fast motion, Ash ducked his head and body, bounced off the lake bottom, kicked his legs, stretched across the open canoe, shoved his upper body out of the water, and grabbed the opposite gunnel. Simultaneously, Moe did the same thing from the other side. Arms stretched across the opening, bodies resting on the gunnels, they clung to the boat. Moe was heavier, and canoe swayed and tilted like it was going to flip over again.

I held my breath.

Moe groaned, "ARRRRR!" and Ash echoed him.

The kids on the beach jumped and chanted, "GO GO GO!"

The canoe bottom lifted high on Ash's side, and then they both landed inside and lay on the canoe's bottom boards. The boat rocked but stayed upright. After a few seconds, Ash stretched both arms overhead and yelled, "ARRRRR!"

The crowd hollered and clapped. Moe laughed, and slapped Ash on the back of his wet lifejacket. Moe's chest heaved, but he paddled back to the beach and showed Ash how to climb out.

Ash staggered through the shallow water and flopped in the sand. For a moment, he lay on his back with both arms stretched over his head. Then he jumped to his feet and bounced in a circle.

Chuckling and shaking his head, Moe hauled the canoe onto the beach. He walked over to Ash and put an arm around his shoulders. "Just saying—kid, you *are* amazing."

"You *are* amazing." Ash echoed Moe's words and tone. Moe raised his hand for a high-five and Ash slapped it so hard, we all heard the smack. Moe clapped and together, they did a victory dance.

"Ash ... you're so strong! There's *no way* I could've handled that canoe without you."

"No way!" Ash flexed his muscles and pretended he had a sword. "Ash is a pirate. Pirates are *strong*!" He shook his arm at the lake and yelled, "ARRRRR!"

At supper time, an electric-pink poster was tacked on the bulletin board outside the cafeteria. The bulletin board was used to update us on camp changes or special events. The Bobcat girls noticed it right away and ran over.

"It's the results from the *SHIVERS!* Audition."

As usual, Rip was the one who kept us informed. I memorized the list of assignments and names to write them in my journal later, with my comments. The list included: Musicians, Dancers, Chorus, Set and Props, Costume, Makeup, Technical Production.

And so on. Tasha was right... everyone had a part. At the bottom of the poster was a list of the major roles. The names I recognized and remembered were: MC – Moe; Lead Pirate/Calico Jack—Grif; Lady Anne—Tasha; Famous Pirate Juggler—Ash; Final Solo-TBD.

I'd figured Grif would get the lead – but Tasha!!!!!

CHOICES

~~~~~~~~~~~~~~~

That evening's campfire was a pep rally to get the camp excited about the *SHIVERS!* production. JB and the counselors organized it like an old-fashioned pantomime show, where the audience yelled at the actors onstage and the actors talked back to the audience. They taught us actions to go with the play.

When I was a little kid, I'd been to a panto; Suzi and Jon were still Mommy and Daddy then. It was such a blast, that afterwards I said I wanted to be an actor. That was the beginning of my performing career. Suzi brought me along when she had gigs and it was fun to join her.

SHIVERS! was supposed to be humorous, with lots of physical comedy and flexibility to allow for when screw-ups happened.

"Actually," Tasha said, "the screw-ups are the best. The more unexpected stuff happens, the better. We get good at improv because we never know what's going to happen."

Each act practiced at the campfire on a separate night. JB's idea was that we'd get confidence with a camp audience before the final show for the parents. The kids in the Bike and Juggling class started the evening's program off.

At the beginning of their routine, Moe rode out on a unicycle. He was hilarious and warmed up the crowd. When the rest of the cyclists and jugglers came out, Ash appeared. He wore a top hat and red suspenders to hold up baggy striped pants. His balance on the bike was incredible. He juggled six plastic bowling pins and didn't drop any. Then he added an apple and managed to catch it in his mouth. The crowd exploded with applause.

After the show I stayed behind, hoping to meet Grif as the crowd filtered away to the cabins. Tasha came up beside me, blocked my path, and stopped. Her eyes narrowed, and her expression was tight.

My inner warning signal went off.

Was Ms. Bossy on to my plans? I hadn't gone anywhere near Grif. I didn't want anyone to gossip about us.

"Do we need to talk?"

Even though I shifted and turned away, she kept going. "Raven, you've been avoiding me recently. In fact, you've still made no effort to connect with *anyone*. The LITs say you never talk to them or want to hang out. Is something going on?"

My face flushed. As it always did, Tasha's directness caught me off guard. She was right, and I was embarrassed. I didn't know the other girls' real names. I hadn't bothered to learn anything about them. I'd given them stupid nicknames.

Yeah. I'd been a jerk.

I had an excuse, even if it wasn't a good one.

When I was on TripleT, fans often followed me around, asking for selfies or my autograph. Once it happened in the grocery store, when I had a box of tampons in my hand. I was afraid of them, especially if there was a group, pulling at my clothes, taking pictures, swarming me. Afraid they'd hurt me.

In those days, I'd learned to lie about my identity, in order to protect myself. I wasn't Viva Tantie. I had an imaginary life— as another girl. Like I'd told Tasha on the first day, I'd invented a girl with siblings and parents who loved her. A girl who was unknown—and safe.

Without thinking, I said, "I've been worried about my family. My sisters and brothers. Mom's been sick." I faked a worried tone.

"Bullshit." The word was like a slap in the face.

Busted. My stomach twisted.

Right. She'd been briefed before I arrived. Of course she knew I was lying.

"You need to stop with the lies." Tasha put her hands on her hips. "What *else* are you lying about, Raven?"

I backed away. "How *dare* you? You don't understand me at all. You only know what other people have said. My parents . . . my therapist . . . did you see all the crap the creeps posted on social media?"

It was the first time I'd *ever* asked anyone that question, and it made me feel sick.

She nodded. "I even watched the show where you crashed."

"And did you laugh your head off?"

"I cried for you."

That was a shock.

No. One. Ever. Cried. For. Me.

"I know everything," she said.

141

My face burned, and my eyes filled with tears.

Tasha didn't know everything.

At first, when I'd run off the TripleT stage, clutching my throat and croaking like a frog, the audience was silent with shock. Then the tsunami started. Behind the curtain, where I'd collapsed on the floor, I heard it. Laughter. The judges' bells clanged, and someone called for an ambulance.

Later, when the hospital tests confirmed my vocal cords had ripped and bled, Suzi'd screamed that I'd been an idiot and ruined everything. Jon swore, and said we should sue TripleT for abuse and mismanagement. Then he remembered that my mother was my manager.

That's when I started therapy with Dr. Hill.

Tasha was quiet, and I started to cry. Big gulping sobs shook my shoulders. When I tried to talk, the words caught in my throat and broke into ugly chunks. Tasha waited it out. My crying was hideous and when the worst was over, I hiccupped. Tears and snot ran down my face.

"You're a mess," she said after a while.

It wasn't meant to be mean and she handed me a tissue. Even when she felt tired and cranky, Tasha lived the 'honest and kind' camp philosophy. She patted my knee.

"Do you need some time alone?" She tilted her head and gazed into my eyes. Her long hair was messy where it had fallen loose from her bun. Back lit by the sun, it was like a frizz of tangled spider webs. Worry lined her sweaty forehead.

I gulped and blew my nose. "You're right, I'm a mess. Sorry!" I tried to laugh, and it came out as a hiccup. "In so many ways! I need to go for a walk and get some fresh air. I won't be too long."

"Sure you're okay? If it would help, I'm happy to stay with you."

"Are you saying that because you're my counselor ... or my friend?"

"Both." She released the hand brake, and put space between us. "Remember, I'm always here for you."

I watched her turn and head towards Bobcat cabin. In the dark, the cabin windows glowed like spotlights. All of the interior lights were on and the shape of a girl appeared at a window. Another silhouette emerged on the porch. The Bobcat girls were waiting for us to come back.

Guilt. Shame. That's how I felt.

Dr. Hill had talked about the importance of identifying my emotions. In my therapy sessions, she'd talked about letting go of the past, learning to love myself and moving forward.

We always have choices, she'd said. *Ask yourself, is this a need ... or a want?*

I wiped my face, took a deep breath and blew my nose. While I fanned my face cool with both hands, I counted to ten.

I scratched a mosquito bite and it made me feel better. My mind cleared. It was time to make a good choice.

I wanted someone to love me.

The choice was simple, because Grif was waiting behind the cafeteria.

GRIF'S SECRETS

~~~~~~~~

When I stepped around the corner of the building, there was a tiny glow in the bushes. It disappeared, and a tall shadow stepped out. I knew it was a human, because bears don't carry phones, and the only person who had a phone (that I knew of) was Grif. He opened his arms wide and stepped forward.

Hey, you."

"Hey yourself." We moved close together. Not touching, but close enough to hear each other breathing.

"I missed you at the beach this afternoon."

He took a few steps back and reached for my hand. "Come with me."

The solar lights along the pathway left pools of light and dark.

He led me towards a bench in one of the unlit spots. A branch had fallen on the path and I stumbled. He caught my arm and asked if I was okay.

After we sat on a bench, he patted my knee and took a deep breath. His hands trembled, and he seemed agitated.

"Grif, are you okay? You seem kinda upset."

He'd always been cocky and super confident, so this wasn't the Grif I thought I knew. But then, I didn't know much about him, really.

"I had a tough meeting with JB today."

"Why?" I waited, eager to show my sympathy.

"The guy's a control freak. He's a do-gooder social worker with a mission to save the world. He bugs me."

He turned away, so I couldn't see his face. This meeting wasn't going the way I expected. And there were questions I needed answers for.

"Grif, before you came to camp this summer, where were you?"

It was a long time before he answered. Behind us in the woods, an owl hooted, and out on the lake a loon called. Even though I recognized it, the sound was eerie. A mosquito buzzed around my head. I had so many bites, I didn't worry; in fact, I welcomed another one.

"I was in rehab." His voice was soft, broken.

"What?"

He didn't reply. He looked at the sky and I followed his gaze. Clouds had rolled in and we couldn't see the moon or stars.

"I need a drink right now. Dying for one."

"Holy crap ... I don't know what to say." I shifted farther away on the bench so we weren't touching. Not to get away from him, but to see his face. Was this real?

"I told some of this at the first campfire, but there's more. I've played basketball since I was a kid. Last year, I made the college team. Mostly watched from the bench because I was first year. At the end of the season, I played in a few games and a tournament. But after I got hurt, I got mixed up in some bad shit." His voice broke.

"I was on an athletic scholarship. When I broke my leg, I was off the team. The pain was unreal. When the meds ran out, I found a way to get more. And booze. Lots of both. I stopped going to class and failed my courses."

I reached for Grif's hand and squeezed it. He took a deep breath and exhaled.

"When they kicked me out, Dad was pissed off. He's got plenty of dough—he could have paid my full way. He's a big time real-estate developer. But it was the prestige of saying, 'my son's at a top college on a basketball scholarship.' I hit rock bottom. Dad took me to a private clinic. I tried so hard to get clean. I want to play next fall, but Dad won't pay my way. Now, he doesn't trust me."

He paused for a breath, and my heart ached for him.

"I'm so sorry." I moved closer, placed my hand on his arm and lightly patted it. "Then what happened?"

"When he heard that a spot had opened here, Dad pulled some strings and got me hired. JB doesn't know we're related. My father hates JB."

"Wow. I had no idea." I edged away from him. My stomach twisted trying to make sense of his story. "Why did you want to come here?"

From the beginning, Grif had been different from the other counselors. Unpredictable at times. And worse. Because I liked him, I wanted to make excuses for him. Then a light went on in my head and I scrambled to my feet. I'd been slow on the uptake. *He'd lied to me.*

"You aren't the camp photographer. You sent fake news to

the media. You and your father want to ruin JB."

He didn't move a muscle. His phone vibrated in his pants' pocket.

"Grif—this is *so* wrong. Why does your dad want to do this? Why are you going along with it?"

He ignored the phone and focused on me.

"There's a good reason why I've done stuff. Because if my dad buys this island, he'll build a theme park. One that everyone can enjoy. He's already installed the communications tower on the mainland for the condo development. If he can get a deal here, he promised to send me back to school."

"Whoa." This was unexpected. I backed away from him. "What about the camp? What about the Owl Lady and the sanctuary? Don't you care about them?"

"Think about it, Raven. Can't you see this place is doomed? The entire camp is run down. Who operates without technology access? JB denies kids the opportunity to connect with the outside world. He doesn't teach business skills, just stuff that's not practical. The people here live in a fantasy world. This whole property should be bulldozed."

He paused and cracked his knuckles. His voice was harsh, angry. I was frozen with shock, and he had more to say.

"The old lady out in the bush has dementia. She's almost blind. JB doesn't take care of her. She'd be safer taking Dad's offer to buy her out. She should move to a long-term care facility on the mainland where she'd get decent supervision and medical support. This is a good deal for everybody!"

He glanced at the ground and then back up at me. "You could help me with this. We've shared a lot of secrets. We could work together."

My head spun. I walked a tight circle around the bench.

"This is so messed up. I thought we met tonight because you cared about me."

He put his hand on my shoulder. "I do. We've both had tough times. We've got a lot in common. If you help me—"

We heard the sound of JB's ATV driving back from the waterfront, and jumped apart.

"I have to go. Tasha and the other girls will wonder where I am."

The ATV was coming closer. Grif's voice was husky. "Okay. Think about it. I really, really, need your help."

I left him, stepped off the path and onto the field, and tried to pick my way across it without being caught by JB. I headed for the cabin lights in the distance.

Behind me, I heard the buzz of a vibrating phone and Grif's low voice answering it.

It didn't take long for JB to find me. He pulled up alongside and turned off the engine.

"Earth-child, you're out late. Hop in, and I'll give you a ride to your cabin."

"Thanks, JB, but I want to walk back. I'm just thinking about things."

"Thinking is good," he said. "And I'd like you to think about something. How'd you like to do the final solo in the show?"

HONESTY AND KINDNESS

~~~~~~~~~

The next morning at breakfast, I made a fool of myself. I was late and on edge, trying to take my mind off Grif and our conversation from the night before. I filled my tray with food, and headed for our table.

Willa was at Grif's table, sitting close beside him, and they were talking low so no one else could hear. Then—CRASH! In front of the entire room, I dropped my tray on the floor. Thankfully, no one laughed, and the kitchen staff helped clean up. The Bear cabin boys had already gone outside. When Willa and Grif left together, he didn't look my way. That hurt.

As usual at meals, Tasha had a heaping plate of food. The day's special was French toast with toasted almonds and blueberry sauce. The other girls from Bobcat cabin had finished and left for their electives. I waited until Tasha's mouth was empty before I asked my question.

"I'm curious. Why does JB want me to do a solo in *SHIVERS!?*"

Tasha stabbed a square of toast and swirled it in the sauce. She brought it to her mouth, then paused.

"Probably someone suggested it. You're still a wonderful singer. He likes someone to do a solo at the end of the camp session. I've heard you sing at the campfire. Your voice is coming back... it's just not the same. Sounds a *little* different to me. It would be good for you to—."

I flipped out and yelled at her, "Ha! What do you know? Are you some kind of expert? Do you have any idea how I feel? How I thought my life was going to turn out?"

When she replied, she was mad.

"I know what I'm talking about, Raven. I've had years of voice training. Do you think just because I'm in a wheelchair, that I can't sing? Or that I thought my life was going to be spent in a wheelchair?"

She waved an arm and knocked a glass of water onto her lap. "Crap!"

I grabbed a napkin to help her dry off and tried to apologize. "Sorry, sorry, sorry, Tasha. I'm a complete jerk. Now, you're mad at me... and I deserve it.

She didn't respond, so I tried again. "Tasha, sometimes I don't think before I speak. It's a big problem for me. I'm working on it." I took a breath and counted to ten. "I've heard you sing. You're good. I thought because you're so committed to arts and crafts that—"

"That what? I couldn't do anything else?"

"I guess I judged without knowing much about you."

"No worries." Tasha pushed away from the table. "Sorry I

150

lost it on you." She blinked, and her eyes were full of tears. "Life's not always easy."

She closed her eyes, exhaled and started again, calmer.

"Raven, you've come a long way here. The show's not a done deal. You don't have to do a solo, if you don't want to. But think about it. Tomorrow you're scheduled for another call with your parents. Can you can handle it better than last time?"

I closed my eyes and shuddered. "That was bad. I don't know what comes over me sometimes. After I do or say stupid stuff, I always regret it." My hand reached for the mosquito bite on my arm.

Tasha grabbed my hand to stop me.

"No more. Quit it. You don't need that anymore. Let it go."

"I can't help it. Something just takes over." The words jammed in my throat and I struggled to speak. Instead of words, broken sounds came out.

Tasha patted my hand and waited until I stopped. She pushed her plate away and took a sip of orange juice. Around us, a team of campers from the Beaver cabin cleaned the tables and stacked the chairs. Two of the campers hovered near our table, willing us to leave.

Tasha leaned against me and put her arm around my shoulder. "We all mess up at times. We have to keep going." Her voice took the preachy tone she sometimes used. "You know my motto ..."

"Yeah. Honesty and kindness."

"It keeps us outta trouble!"

She'd took another gulp of juice and finished eating. I reached over and lifted her tray from our table.

"Tasha, meeting you is the best thing that's ever happened to me. I mean it."

"Thanks. I try, but I'm far from perfect. Just working on it!" She laughed and smoothed back her frizzy hair. "There's a storm coming soon. My hair feels it and so do my bones. How's your schedule going? Rehearsals ... swim team?" She raised one eyebrow.

I took a moment to think, as we dropped off her tray and headed for the exit. I surprised myself. "It's great. Dancing and singing again feels good. It's like I belong. I'm learning to swim— and I love fooling around with the kayaks and canoes. I'm not an expert, but I'm improving."

"Good. What about the boy who arrived the same day as you? Ash. Have you spent any time with him?"

It had been a few days since I'd connected with Ash and for some strange reason, it made me feel guilty. I wondered how his owl was doing.

"Maybe during this afternoon's free time, we could visit the Owl Lady? He wants to see that bird before it flies away."

"That's a good plan. I'll talk to Moe and see if he's okay with it. I'm sure he'll agree this is important."

"I've got another question. What's with JB and his mother, the Owl Lady? What happened between them?"

"You and your tough questions."

I held the door for Tasha and she followed me outside. She stretched, shrugged her shoulders and shook her head.

"None of us know what happened. They used to be close. They even sang together. I heard that he helped her with the Sanctuary. After he started touring with his band, he didn't come to the island. It broke her heart. They drifted apart. He's sad about it. I guess that's why he gives everyone a second chance."

"And the red-noses?"

"After he met Kirra, he worked with kids in hospitals. The two of them never had kids of their own. One day at a cancer clinic, he dressed as a clown—not the scary type—but in white makeup and a red-nose. He was gentle. The kids loved him. He's practiced that magic ever since with the camp."

SECOND CHANCES

~~~~~~~~~

After Tasha left for her craft class, I thought about her words. The ideas stayed with me in dance class and I made mistakes in the routine I usually aced.

At the dock, during yoga, Willa called my name twice to put out the mats before I realized she was talking to me. I couldn't concentrate on the stretches, too full of confusing thoughts and too aware of Grif out in the lake, teaching someone to swim.

Moe and Ash found me after the class and said they'd spent the morning paddling on the lake. Ash bounced on his toes. Moe gave him a high-five and turned to me.

"Tasha said that this afternoon you want to take Ash back to the Owl Lady. Fantastic!"

153

He turned to Ash. "Buddy, you've worked so hard. You're doing great. And I know you want to see the bird fly. Do you want to go with Raven?"

"See Blackbird. Raven too."

Moe gave Ash a knuckle-bump. "I've cleared it with JB. Thanks for taking him, Raven."

For the first time, Ash made eye contact. "Thanks, Raven. Meet at the trail. See you later." His tone was clipped and mechanical, but the meaning was clear.

When we met, I'd assumed he was like a little kid, but now he acted older . . . more mature. He was almost as tall as me, and his arms had long, well-developed muscles.

"Deal." I raised my hand for a high-five and Ash slapped it.

"Deal," he said.

I took the path to Bobcat cabin to change my clothes. Before I arrived, a familiar voice called my name.

"Raven, wait!" Grif ran so fast he bounced ahead before he stopped. He reversed to face me and bent over, hands on his knees. "Whew! Outta breath. Listen—I've missed you. Everything okay between us?"

He held out a hand and I took it. I hadn't forgotten his words. Some of it made sense. Like me, he'd been through a lot.

JB's right, everyone deserves a second chance.

"More than okay."

He smiled, and I was hooked.

"I heard you're taking that nut-bar kid to see the batty old woman this afternoon."

I was uncomfortable with the way he talked about Ash, and the Owl Lady, but didn't say anything. It was good to have Grif close, and maybe he didn't mean it. Grif goofed around all the time.

He whispered in my ear. "I've got a surprise. I wanted to wait until your birthday tomorrow ... sweet Sixteen! But now's the right time. You should have it before you leave for the Sanctuary. Meet me at the café in a few minutes. You're gonna love it!"

I went to the cafeteria, which was empty except for us, and Grif handed me the best present I could have asked for.

My phone.

My knees felt weak, and I sat on a chair.

"But why? How did you get it?" I tripped over my words.

"I went to the main office last night, trying to find a first aid kit for the Bear cabin, and the safe under Kirra's desk was open. I saw an envelope with your name and took it out. It wasn't stealing—it belongs to you, and I'm returning it to you."

I didn't know what to say.

"I've got a new idea. We're not doing anything wrong. I want you to take photos for an important photography contest. To show the natural environment. If we win the contest, there'd be enough money to preserve the camp and Rainbow Island for the future."

"Wow." I turned the phone. It felt strange holding it after so long. "What do I have to do?"

"Take photos of the Owl Lady's house and property, then send them to me. Don't show anyone else. If we win the contest, everyone will be happy."

Cook walked in before I answered, and I hid the phone in my pocket. Grif left for the waterfront, and I ran to Bobcat cabin.

Even after I wrote in my journal, I worried about his plan. If I left the phone in the cabin, an LIT might find it, and think I was the rat who leaked bad news. I wrapped the phone in a scarf to disguise it, and put it in the front pocket of my jean jacket.

155

The flies were bad on the trail to the sanctuary, so it would seem natural if I wore it.

But then what?

THE RIGHT MOMENT TO LEAVE

Ash and Moe were waiting at the trail entrance to the Sanctuary when I arrived. It was stinking hot, there was thunder in the distance, and dark clouds rolled across the waterfront from the direction of the mainland.

"I dunno, Raven. Looking at the sky, we're in for bad weather. I know Ash is excited, but maybe you should wait until tomorrow. When the storm blows over."

Ash's mouth dropped. "No No NO!" His voice got louder with each 'no.' He waved at the clouds and pointed at the trail. "Storm blows over. Too late."

Moe shrugged and glanced at me. "Raven, do you need that jacket? I'm sweating standing here."

I wondered if Moe saw the bulge of my phone in my pocket. Beads of sweat trickled down my back and broke out on my forehead. Ash's hands flapped, and he bounced in place.

"I'm not hot. The jacket keeps the bugs off. I've been wondering about the owl, and Ash really, really wants to go. It's probably almost ready to fly now."

"Okay. JB knows where you are. If bad weather rolls in, he'll come with the quad. Good luck!"

Moe left, and Ash ran ahead along the lane towards the Owl Lady's shack. I noticed tire tracks in the dirt, and I wondered if JB secretly drove in to check on his mother.

The trail didn't seem as long or difficult as before. But the flies were as bad, and they dive bombed my head. Nasty little blood suckers. I yanked my ball cap low and pulled my jacket collar to cover my neck. For the first time in months, I missed having long hair.

Nothing bothered Ash. He charged ahead, but whenever he felt too far away, turned around and ran back to me. He didn't see me take photos. When he reached the top of the hill, he waited. We leaned on the fence and watched the beaver pond. A line of sweat snaked along my backbone, and I used my hat as a fan to cool myself. Just like the last time, a beaver swam across the pond. Its head appeared, cutting a trail on the surface. When it reached the lodge, it splashed its tail and disappeared.

A raven cawed overhead. When I first arrived on the island, the animal noises terrified me. I was still paranoid about bears. I'd overheard senior counselors talk about the animals the Owl Lady had treated and released over the years. They'd said the cages on her property used to be full. In emergencies, a vet from the mainland came over by boat. She got her nickname from a pet owl that flew around and pooped on the furniture.

I didn't tell anyone about Percy, her skunk.

Ash ran ahead, but disappeared into the bushes behind the outhouse. I grabbed a few more photos and decided to go inside that nasty little building again. At least I knew there wasn't a bear hiding in the back. When I heard the rustles, I wasn't scared. We left together and headed for the Owl Lady's shack.

The sound of a noisy engine made us both stop and listen. It didn't sound like JB's vehicle.

Without waiting for me, Ash ran ahead. I took a few fast photos, shoved the phone back in my pocket and followed.

In the distance, a man in a black quad pulled away from the Owl Lady's shack. He wheeled the machine around and left by a back way that I hadn't noticed before. A dusty cloud hung in the air behind him. We didn't see the Owl Lady, but her front door was open.

Ash tried to head inside.

"Wait!" I grabbed his hand.

"She invited us!" He shook my hand away but stopped and to listen.

"Ash, we can't just barge inside. That's friggin' rude. She doesn't know we're coming. We might scare her. What if she's asleep?"

I honestly didn't think she was sleeping. But someone else had been visiting. Who? My stomach twisted. Why would anyone be there? My phone vibrated but I ignored it. There was only one person who'd try to reach me, and I wasn't sure I wanted to talk to him.

Ash banged his fist against the front wall of the shack. The old lady didn't answer.

"Try again."

He knocked a second time. Still no one.

"Hello?" I pushed her door open wider and called inside.

Ash echoed my words.

"Hello? Mrs. Owl Lady ... are you home?

From somewhere inside a faint voice responded. "Come in."

I held my breath. It was dim, so I couldn't see much. I blinked and waited until my eyes adjusted and I saw a dark shape lying on the couch.

"Who is it? JB, is that you?" Her voice was weak, almost inaudible.

Percy slithered by and ran out the open door. There was a thump near the back wall, by her wood stove.

"It's Raven and Ash. Remember, we brought you the owl? You told us to come back, so here we are." I knelt beside her and Ash copied me.

She tried to sit, but didn't have the strength. There was a flattened red pillow under her head. She wore a blue flowered dress with a long skirt that covered her skinny legs. Short leather boots, worn and scuffed at the toes and heels, were still on her feet. I took a deep breath and tried to sound calm so I wouldn't scare Ash.

"Is something wrong? Can I get you anything?" My nerves were on edge. It was scary, because I wasn't used to sick people. Or people that were ancient. She was as helpless, and what was the word—as discombobulated—as the little owl was.

"It's been a busy day. I'm just resting." She patted my jacket sleeve. "But if you could loosen my shoes, I'd be grateful."

I untied her laces and slid the boots off her feet and tried not to gag. Whew! Her feet stunk. Underneath the boots, she wore a pair of multi-coloured striped socks with holes in the toes and heels.

"Is that better?" I dropped the boots on the floor and took a short, quick breath. The banging got louder and faster.

Ash wandered around the room. Snooping. He followed the weird noise to the woodstove, then dropped to his hands and knees.

"Blackbeard!" He crawled into a gap, slid a big cage out from the back, and put his face close to the owl.

"You're the twins." The old lady mumbled, so I placed my ear close to her face to hear what she was saying. "I'm glad you're back. That Great Horned Owl is ready to release. Take the bird outside into a clearing, and open the cage. Then move back to let it out. This might take a while. You'll have to wait for just the right moment. It's strong enough to be free."

Ash needed no more encouragement to haul the cage fully out. He grunted and muttered to himself, when it got wedged between the stove and couch.

"Don't give up when things get hard." The Owl Lady closed her eyes. "After the owl flies away, come back and have a chat. I had an unpleasant visitor today. I need a little rest."

Ash was strong, but the cage was awkward to carry, and the swinging motion frightened the owl. The bird crashed around the bottom and fluttered its wings against the wire walls. Ash put his hand inside to try to calm it. Beak open, the owl lashed out at him. Its talons curled and tried to slash his fingers. Ash squealed, yanked his hand back, and his sleeve snagged on a cage wire.

He was stuck. I grabbed the cage with one hand to steady it.

"Let me help you," I said, and instantly regretted it. When I slipped my free hand through an open section to release his shirt, the owl attacked. It stabbed my fingers with its beak. The pain was sharp. I yelped, and let go. The cage slipped out of my grip.

Because his sleeve was still caught, Ash held on, but he tripped over the coffee table. When he fell, the crash shook the room. The cage rolled onto its side, and the bird fell on its back and lay still.

Ash yanked his shirt loose and started to moan.

"It's dead! I killed it." He rolled into a fetal position and lay on his side, sobbing and rocking.

It was disturbing, because he hadn't acted like that before. I'd seen him upset, but never seen him that distraught. Then I remembered the times he'd run away, and the problem with the life-jacket. He'd come so far, but had he lost every gain? *Was this my fault?*

My hand throbbed. Then I saw bright red and almost fainted. Blood spurted out of my finger and ran along my palm and wrist. Either the bird's beak or a piece of rusted cage wire had cut me.

During the commotion, the Owl Lady pushed herself upright and staggered to her feet. She sounded annoyed. "You people are noisy. What's all the racket? Settle down. You've scared the owl."

She was right, the bird was freaked out. Despite the pain and my shakes, I tried to pull myself together. The young owl huddled in a corner of the cage, unharmed, but terrified. It's large yellow eyes were wider than ever and its feathers were all fluffed out. It seemed twice as large as when we found it. Then it made a noise.

Hoot . . . hoot. Softly at first, then louder, as if it was warning us to keep away.

When the owl hooted, Ash lifted his head and uncurled his body. He crawled over to the cage and stared through the wire at the bird. Then he hooted back. The owl blinked and its feathers settled.

In a no-nonsense tone, the Owl Lady said, "Dear, your hand is dripping blood on my floor. Go to the sink in the kitchen and wash it off. Use soap."

"Wash off. Use soap." Without a change in his position, Ash echoed her words.

The old lady bent over the cage and cooed. "Aren't these people ridiculous? And so messy. You'll have to wait for the girl to stop bleeding. Then her brother will take you outside and set you free. There's a nice hollow tree in the woods that's perfect for you. And lots of yummy red squirrels to catch."

I was dizzy, and my finger felt like it had been stabbed with a sword. But complaining about it wasn't going to win any sympathy from those two. I had to take care of myself. At the old woman's deep kitchen sink, I scrubbed away the blood and rubbed a bar of yellow soap over my hands and on my arms. It smelled like the disinfectant at a hospital.

If the TripleT makeup crew could see me now, they'd faint. No one can ever call me a wimp again.

The cut wasn't deep and the cold water from her rusty tap eased the throbs. After the blood washed down the drain, I searched for a towel to dry my hands and noticed a collection of prescription pill bottles on the window ledge. They were all empty.

Hung on the wall was an old-fashioned telephone with a loopy cord. I'd never seen one before. Beside it, taped on the faded wallpaper was a handwritten list of phone numbers. I wrapped a clean-looking dish towel around my hand and studied them. The numbers were for a doctor, a veterinarian, and for JB.

When I returned to the living room, Ash had cleared a path through the furniture, so he could carry the cage outside. The Owl Lady walked behind, encouraging him.

I ran to the door to open it for them. Outside in the sunlight, Ash and the Owl Lady stood still and waited, while the bird flopped around in the cage, fluttering its wings. She took a firm hold of my arm and pointed behind the shack.

"Take the owl to the middle of that clearing, open the cage and stand back. Let it take some time." The Owl Lady clasped her hands together and pulled them to her chest, like she was going to pray. "You two go on ahead. I'm slow. This has been a tremendously stressful day. I'm not used to this much company."

Ash and I walked around the back of the house. It must have been a graveled parking lot when the sanctuary operated, but long grass, daisies and wildflowers had taken over. An overgrown dirt road led through a meadow and disappeared into the forest. The mystery man in the ATV had travelled out that way.

Ash went ahead and placed the cage on a flat spot. Before opening it, he came back to me. I didn't think we should be close when the cage opened, in case the owl attacked. Even inside the cage, when it jumped around or stared at us, it gave me the creeps.

"Say something, Raven." Ash swayed back and forth, as if he expected a ceremonial speech.

"Like what?"

"Say goodbye. Tell the bird to fly. Take the broken wings into the sky."

"You've been listening to Moe too much," I said. He didn't respond, and I felt ashamed for poking fun at him. "Okay, I get it...you mean the song the Owl Lady taught us."

Ash nodded. "I sing too."

I looked around. We were in the middle of nowhere. If I sang and messed up, nobody would know. At first my voice was soft and squeaky. I tried some of the words of the Blackbird song. Ash didn't care how it sounded. He joined in and sang the words without mistakes.

It wasn't a sudden miracle. We didn't sound fantastic. He was stiff, I was unsteady. No recording company would offer a contract. When we finished, he raised his hand in a salute and stood like a statue. Above us, the sky was dark with fast-moving storm clouds, and thunder rolled over the lake. The storm was close.

"You better hurry. It will rain soon." The Owl Lady was so quiet, we hadn't noticed her. She was still in her socks. "Lovely singing, my dears. Young man, last week on the phone, I told

Kirra that your sister should sing in the show." She pointed at me.

Why did she keep saying that? It was annoying, every time. Before I could correct her, Ash took giant steps, like a mechanical marching soldier, over to the cage. The owl was hunched in a corner, fluffed to twice its size, with its big yellow eyes opened wide. He knelt on the ground, released the latch and opened the door. The old lady raised her voice.

"Get back. Let the poor little thing choose its time."

Ash moved away and stood beside me. The owl flattened its feathers, and took a tentative hop forward towards the opening. I held my breath. It hopped again and fluttered its wings to lift itself to the edge of the door. After another hop, it landed in the dirt outside the cage.

"Shhhh." Ash put his finger over his lips. "Be very quiet. Noise scares babies."

The owl hesitated and swiveled its head. It spread its wings and shook them. Then it lifted, and fluttered a few feet above the ground. After a short flight, it landed in the tall grass on the other side of the drive.

"Didn't fly away." Ash was astounded. "Why?"

The Owl Lady put a shaky hand on his shoulder. "It takes time to learn how. The owl's going to be fine. It'll practice it again and again. Watch!" She pointed at the owl. Blackbeard spread its wings, flapped and lifted out of the grass. It flew a few feet higher, then soared over to a section of fencing and landed on a post. Its head swiveled over its shoulder in our direction.

And then it blinked.

The thunder boomed louder and the rumbles were close together. A vein of lightning split the sky. The leaves of the trees rattled in the breeze. The Owl Lady pulled her sweater tighter across her chest. "If that storm gets worse, that fella will have trouble crossing the lake. You should never be out in a boat during a thunderstorm."

"You mean the guy who was here before we arrived?" I peered down the back road into the forest.

"He wants my property. He wants to buy the entire island. He said JB doesn't take good care of me. When JB was naughty, I got angry with him. Once I thought about selling and moving to the mainland. But what would happen to all the animals that live here? What would happen to Blackbird?"

She coughed and swayed on her feet. "I need to call JB and straighten things out before this goes too far. That fella's in a big hurry and is pushing me too fast. You two head back to the camp before the storm hits. I'm going inside to ask JB to come for a cup of tea. It's been a long time since he's had any of my cookies."

We turned to say goodbye. The thunder and lightning made Ash anxious, so he started to rock back and forth, and flap his fingers. The Owl Lady leaned a moment against her doorframe, a tiny frail shape with raspy breathing. Then she stepped inside and closed the door.

As Ash headed down the lane, I waited a moment, took the phone out and tried to frame a few good pictures. The coming storm, the overgrown fields, the broken barn, her messy house, the empty cages, the road that led away.

Even though I felt uneasy, I got it all.

SELF-CONTROL

~~~~~~~~

We ran so hard, I thought I was going to be sick. My lungs burned, so I yelled at Ash to slow down and wait. He wouldn't stop. We heard the storm coming nearer every second. Crashes, followed by flashes of lighting that lit the sky. Ash decided we were being chased by pirates and screamed at them to stay back. I couldn't tell if he was serious or pretending.

My jacket made me so hot, I wanted to take it off. When the phone banged against my left boob, I worried about the photos I'd taken for Grif. What did he plan to do with them, anyway? What if he'd lied to me, and wanted to post them online with derogatory comments. Humiliate the Owl Lady?

No, that's absurd. It was for a contest that could win money

167

for the camp.

Ash pointed at dark blobs on the dirt path ahead. The rain began and I tucked the phone away before he noticed. When Moe met us, it was pouring. As the three of us ran to our cabins, Ash yelled that he needed a sword to fight the crocodiles.

By the time I reached Bobcat cabin, I was soaked and headed straight for the shower. The Bobcat girls were quiet when I came in, but Squeak turned away from me and giggled. It made me a little mad.

As the hot water poured onto my skin, I thought about my parents. Our next phone call was after dinner, before the campfire show. I was ashamed of what had happened last time, but I was still mad at them. But the yoga and meditation classes had helped me develop self-control. I was sure it would go better.

I turned off the tap and watched the water run down the drain, between my toes.

BIRTHDAYS AND BABIES

~~~~~~~~~~

The rain lasted about thirty minutes. By the time I'd toweled off, changed, and dried my hair, the sun was out. The LITs had already left for supper, so I walked over by myself. Out over the lake, there was another rainbow. This time, there was no one around, so I stopped and listened.

In the trees, the breeze rustled the overhead branches, and the red squirrel chattered. In the forest, a woodpecker drilled holes in a tree, farther out an owl hooted. Maybe it was Blackbird.

But the sound of a rainbow? Nothing.

When I found them, the Bobcat girls and Tasha were at our table with their heads together, laughing and whispering. Rip spotted me come across the room and pulled on Stick's arm to make her stop. They went quiet and blushed. When I sat beside her, Squeak giggled.

"What's the big secret?" I placed my dinner tray on an empty spot beside Tasha. She shifted her chair over to make room, so I could sit between Spex and her.

"The show! Tasha told us what it's like to rehearse with Grif. She said he's a terrible singer and can't act."

"I didn't say that!" Tasha rolled her eyes. "Don't misquote me. I said, his best talents are playing basketball and breaking girl's hearts. That was mean, so I'm sorry."

"Whose heart did he break?" I wanted to sound disinterested. I wound a strand of spaghetti into a ball on my fork and rolled it across my plate.

"Willa, for one. She's nuts about him. And all the girls he's supposedly teaching to swim. Half of them already know how; they fake it. He holds them and pretends he's helping them float." Spex smirked.

I lost my appetite. I took a sip of ice tea, and mashed the spaghetti ball into a stringy pancake.

"And you, too, Raven. You like him. We can tell," said Rip.

Tasha's eyes were sympathetic when she defended me.

"We *all* think he's hot. The guy's a ten. Admit it, you all watch him. And lucky me gets to play opposite him in the show." She pushed her plate away and pointed at the servery. "I'm hungry for dessert. They set out stuff for banana splits. Could someone get me one?"

The Bobcat girls went to the ice-cream dispenser. Beside it, dressed in aprons and chef's hats, were the kids who rode the ferry with me.

As we waited at the table, Tasha and I watched the helpers dump soft ice-cream into large bowls. They handed out sliced bananas, chocolate or caramel sauce, and chopped walnuts.

Big-Boy was last in the lineup with a can of whipped cream in his hand. He topped the concoctions with a swirled white pyramid and a maraschino cherry. It was two-thousand calories of incredible deliciousness. Even Stix, who never ate dessert, took one.

Tasha met my eyes. "No dessert? You okay?"

"I guess. I'm skipping dessert because I have to go to the office. I've got an appointment with my parents. Hope this one goes better."

"I remember. Want me to come with you?"

"Nah. Kirra talked to me earlier today. I'm first again so I can get to the campfire early. JB wants us to bring the red-noses and practice wearing them. Sanjay will take promo pictures for the website to let the parents see us prepare for the show."

"Okay. Remember, if you need backup ... I'm in your corner."

My eyes filled with tears. "Thanks." I took my plate over to the compost bucket, scraped my plate and headed for the office.

When I arrived, Ash was already there. Moe sat beside him, sharing a magazine and pointing out pictures. The conversation was stilted, but Ash spoke in short sentences. Again, I realized how much he'd changed. I hadn't seen the harness and leash since camp began.

When I sat beside them, Ash said, "Raven helped let Blackbeard go. We sang a lullaby. Babies like lullabies. I'm going to sing to our new baby."

Moe glanced sideways at me and shrugged in an *I dunno...* kind of way. Sometimes, Ash still didn't make any sense.

Kirra came in the room carrying a chart, then checked her computer screen. "Raven, you're next. Ash goes after you, and then Sanjay will help the others." She shook her candy bowl and held it out to us. Ash jumped and grabbed a handful. Had she got rid of the ones that fell on the floor? I wasn't sure they were fresh, so I smiled and said no thanks.

Kirra studied her screen again, then grinned. "Someone's having a special day soon. Happy Birthday, Raven!"

I felt my face turn red. "It's not until tomorrow."

"I know. But I might not see you and wanted to wish you all the best. I remember my sixteenth birthday. So long ago ... it's such a great age." She went back to her computer.

Sanjay opened the Infirmary door and gestured to me. I wandered into the tech office, sat in the padded chair and stared at the dark monitor.

"I'll be outside and won't be part of the call unless you need me. Oh... and Happy Birthday for tomorrow!"

"Thanks." My voice was small, and I wasn't sure he heard me. I stared at the screen and watched two blurry shapes turn into boxes with my parents' heads. Neither one said a word. They both smiled, as if waiting to be interviewed for a television show. They'd probably discussed our messy last call, and neither one wanted to set off another disaster.

I broke the ice. "Hey guys! How's it going?" I arranged my facial features into a smile of 'charming innocence'. That's what the director called the expression I learned to fake in show biz.

Suzi started first. "Sweetheart, you look great! You've got a beautiful tan and I love your hair."

Typical. Appearances were always important to my mom.

"You look good, too, Suzi. Is that a new outfit?"

She fussed with her hair and necklace. "Yes. There was money left over from the sale of the Beamer and the purchase of our new car. I did some back-to-school shopping for you. You'll love the cute outfits I found."

"Sure." *Didn't she realize I was old enough to choose my own clothes?* We stared at each other, already out of conversation.

It was Jon's turn to talk.

"Have you made any new friends? Met some nice kids there?" He had a cheery tone to his voice that made me suspicious.

I hesitated. "Yeah, I have. I like the senior counselors. Especially Tasha. You'd like her too."

"That's good, sweetheart. I'm happy for you." He stopped talking. His eyebrows raised and eyes widened. Then he attempted a smile, but it wasn't happy. He was either hopeful or worried. "I have some great news and I want you to be happy for me."

"Have you found a new home for you and what's-her-name? I'm happy if you have."

"Mia. That's her name. Mia." He cleared his throat. "We have. It's a place for the entire family. Four bedrooms."

"That sounds huge. There's just two of you. Why do you need four bedrooms?"

"Well ..." He ducked his head as if searching for the words. Then he straightened and faced the camera. "We're getting married. She already has a son, but we're expecting a baby."

"What!" Before I could react, Suzi screamed. "Another kid? You're out of your mind! What's that woman thinking? When I saw her at the ferry, I had to leave! Doesn't she have enough on her hands already? Asp or whatever his name is... he's enough!"

The office temperature dropped. Even though it was August, it felt like an arctic wind had blown in. The overhead lights and the screen flickered, and I remembered a storm was coming.

I was stunned. Had I heard wrong?

My father was marrying Ash's mother? Ohmigod! CRASH! The entire camp business was a set-up!

My inside monster roared to life.

Betrayed!

173

The monster flew into a rage, and took over.

"I hate you! Both of you! You've wrecked my life!" The words burst out of my mouth. I'd never said words like that before, but at that moment, I didn't care.

My parents stopped talking and their faces disappeared from the monitor. The overhead lights turned off and the office went dark. The electric power was out, and I couldn't move.

Sanjay opened the door from the infirmary and called, "Don't worry, Raven. We have a generator for electricity. It'll kick in soon—"

Before he finished the sentence, a motor roared outside the building. All the lights flickered, the equipment beeped and turned on, but my conference call had shut down.

"We have the WiFi back now. It's a strong signal. Do you want me to reconnect so you can talk to your parents? It won't take a second."

Sanjay was trying to be helpful, but I wanted none of it.

"I'm done. Bring Ash in. It's his turn to talk. His mom has big news for him. She's getting married and having a new baby."

Staggering like a Zombie in a video game, I left the building. It was too much.

I ran to Bobcat cabin, grabbed my journal and poured my feelings out. I wrote every horrible word I could think of—scribbled them out—then blasted my parents. I felt as bad as I had six months before.

Maybe worse.

Finally, I wrote, *They didn't even wish me Happy Birthday. They don't even care.*

I pulled the covers over my head, curled into a ball and cried myself to sleep.

SECOND THOUGHTS

~~~~~~~~~~

In the morning, I needed a coffee, preferably a strong one. The moment I walked into the cafeteria, I smelled it brewing. No one stopped me, so I wandered into the kitchen. The kids who'd come over on the Poseidon with me were working behind the counter, cooking breakfast at the industrial stove.

Big-Boy cracked eggs into a gadget that resembled a mini tennis racket suspended over a metal bowl. The egg whites dripped through and he dumped the yolks into another bowl. He was counting aloud and finished at fifty.

"That's a lot of eggs."

He nodded and lifted the tool. Gobs of yellow slime dripped off.

"At least I had this. It's hard to separate eggs by hand without

175

messing up or adding shell. I'm baking angel food cakes today, and the yolks can't mix with the whites. It wrecks the batter."

"I LOVE angel food cake!"

He blushed and took a fresh cloth to wipe away the gooey spills on the counter. I glanced at the empty cardboard egg cartoons, and the bags of flour and sugar he'd organized. Without meeting my eyes, he slid all the ingredients over to the food mixer. He was shy and kind and I realized I'd never given him a second thought.

"What's your name?"

"Bren. I already know that you're Raven." He glanced up but avoided meeting my eyes. "Hope you have a great day today." He covered his mouth with his hand, and the flaming blush on his cheeks spread to his ears.

I took a clean white mug from a pile, and poured a cup of coffee, thinking I'd drink it black. Like Suzi did in the morning, when she'd pulled an overnighter working for TripleT. When I took a sip, the coffee burnt my mouth and tasted bitter. I wanted to spit it out, but the rest of the kitchen crew had turned to watch me. The two girls put their heads together and whispered.

"This coffee needs some cream." Just a few drops remained in the little pitcher, so I handed it over to Bren for a refill, and added three teaspoons of sugar to it. "I came to talk to Grif. Is he here?"

Cook came out of the pantry closet carrying a bag of flour in his arms. When he noticed me, his mouth made an O and then snapped shut. "Grif likes to sleep in. This guy—", Cook pointed at Bren, "wants to be a chef, so he comes prepared to learn."

He set the flour on a cleared spot on the steel counter and rubbed his hands together. "Bren's doing fantastic. He's got natural talent."

Bren's face brightened. He tied on a clean apron, took a carton of cream from the frig and filled the container I'd emptied. For the first time, as he passed it to me, our eyes met.

His voice was soft and low. "I didn't see you at the campfire last night, Raven."

"I wasn't feeling well. Stayed back at the cabin." I leaned against the counter, added more cream and took another sip. Better. The cream and sugar took the edge off and it was cooler. "How'd it go?"

"Cool! Moe led the program because JB was away somewhere. Moe was so funny. The gymnastics group did an incredible demo. They've got a big number in the final show. I can't wait ..."

"Yeah. Me neither."

"Everyone wore their camp shirt and we practiced a song with the red-noses. Mine fell off and by accident, I stepped on it. I gotta get another one for the final." The timer on the oven beeped so Bren turned away to remove a tray of fresh baking.

Cook watched as the hot buns were placed on metal cooling racks. He poured himself a coffee.

"You usually don't come by this early in the morning, Raven. Everything okay? Breakfast won't be ready for another thirty minutes."

"I'm just restless. Couldn't sleep last night. Can't wait to get going on another exciting day." My acting training paid off. He couldn't tell that I was lying right to his face.

Even though I was hurting, the smell of Bren's tray of fresh cinnamon buns was divine. Cook gave my shoulder a teeny squeeze, grabbed a clean plate and placed a bun in the centre. He stepped back as the tiny girl walked over with a bowl of fresh made icing. She swirled a glob on the caramel coloured bun. The icing melted, slid down the side and pooled on the dish. She spooned a second glob on top, then brought it over to me.

"Here you go, Raven. I gave you extra icing, because it's so hot, it's melting." Her high-pitched voice was kind. "I hope you like it."

I sat alone at the Bobcat table, sipped the coffee and used a finger to wipe the melted icing on my plate. While I licked my fingers, I thought about my options. I'd been awake most of the night, using every swear word I knew.

I'd created new combinations of profanity for my mother. Suzi hadn't changed one bit while I was away. Totally selfish. All she talked about was clothes and hair. She didn't ask how I was doing.

And Jon. Ohmigod. What an actor he'd turned out to be. And manipulative. That bombshell he'd dropped on my lap! There weren't enough curse words in the world to describe how I felt about his betrayal. My parents had pretended they sent me to camp for therapy. But in reality, they knew I'd meet Ash. And that's why his mother—Mia—thought she recognized me on the first day. That's why my mother wouldn't ride over on the ferry with me.

It dawned on me that they'd been part of a conspiracy. So were JB and Kirra ... and apparently Tasha. They'd all been briefed on my background and my parents' plans.

The coffee twisted in my stomach.

Grif had figured out who I was. Why did everyone in the kitchen whisper when I walked in the door? They all knew my name. We'd never talked to each other before. Did the entire camp know about me? I had a worse thought.

Had they all watched the videos of my breakdown?

I was lost in dark thoughts and jumped when a voice said, "Morning, Sunshine. Another great day ... is headed our way. That bun looks nice ... let's go back twice."

Moe and Ash stood beside me. With one hand, Moe sipped a coffee, but held an oversized key in the other.

At the far side entrance of the room, the Bobcat cabin girls walked in and headed for the breakfast buffet line. They glanced at me, put their heads together, and whispered. Tasha came in behind them, waving when she saw me.

"What's with the key, Moe?"

"We're goin' over to Treasure Island today to search for a hidden box of gold."

"Pirate treasure!" Ash was excited and bounced on his toes. "Pieces of silver! ARRRRR!"

"Fantastic." Sarcasm dripped from my voice, and Moe's smile melted as fast as the icing on the hot bun. "Sorry. I didn't mean to sound like that. I had a migraine last night, and I still don't feel so great."

"We missed you at the campfire. Hope you feel better soon." He grinned at Ash and lifted his eyebrows in mock excitement. "Let's go-go-go, Ash! Don't be a twiddle-waddle. To get to Treasure Island, you've gotta set up your paddle."

The Bobcat girls arrived in a giggling mob and settled around our table. Stix had a huge cinnamon bun on her plate. She sliced it open, cut it into tiny pieces, stabbed them with her chopsticks, and swirled them in the melted butter on her plate.

The others bent over and ate, chatted about their day's plans and how the rehearsals were progressing.

"We missed you last night," Rip said. "When we came back from the campfire, you were huddled under your blanket, sound asleep. We were quiet so we wouldn't bother you. Are you feeling better now?"

From out of nowhere, my conscience reminded me I didn't know her name, just the mean nickname I'd given her. When they'd come back from campfire, I'd been awake, but had faked being asleep so I didn't have to talk to them.

"I'm fine—thanks. My period started, so I don't feel great.

I want to skip my classes this morning. Do something different for a change."

Tasha's eyes narrowed. She licked the icing on her lips. "Like what?" Her voice was tense, like her inner warning alarm had gone off.

"I want to go to Treasure Island. Hunt for hidden treasure with Moe and Ash. Okay?"

Tasha's shoulders relaxed. It was hard to fool her, but maybe I had.

"We're supposed to be rehearsing... but I'll check with JB to see if it's okay. Today's a special event for Grif's high ropes class on the island's Obstacle Course. They're taking the canoes and kayaks over. When they're finished, there's a picnic lunch on the beach."

"Perfect. That's the kind of day I need."

Tasha followed the path to the waterfront with me, and blabbed on and on about the obstacle course. She'd ridden the pontoon boat over to the island several times, but couldn't handle the pathways when she got there. She'd had to stay on the boat and watch the others.

"That sucks," I said. "Maybe JB will find a way to make it more accessible."

"Doubt it. Not unless a miracle happens, and he gets more money. The camp's in trouble."

The asphalt paving ran out before it reached the beach, and the path turned into heavy sand. When Tasha couldn't go any farther, we stopped and watched the kids get organized for Treasure Island. The canoes and kayaks waited along the beach, ready to load. On the beach, a senior counselor helped the campers, and another counselor floated in a canoe off shore.

Tasha sighed and wiped sweat from her forehead. "I want to get a new chair in the fall." She adjusted her position and tied her frizzy hair back in a ponytail. "I've applied to get one with better wheels for rough terrain. With a motor. Kind of like JB's ATV, but just for me."

"I didn't see JB at breakfast. I heard he wasn't at the campfire last night."

"He's with the Owl Lady. First thing this morning, Kirra held a meeting for the senior counselors. She said his mother phoned yesterday, saying she had chest pains. JB took off in the quad. He didn't come back last night. A doctor's coming this afternoon. Kirra called JB to approve your trip to Treasure Island. I told them you needed a break, and I support it."

"Oh." It took me a moment to respond. "I hope the Owl Lady's okay."

Tasha shrugged. "I dunno. The two of them have been estranged for a long time. They must have had a big fight. I don't know the whole story. Kirra said he's worried about his mother's health and the way she lives. But his mother doesn't want him to come on the property. Contacting JB to ask him to come over is a sign that her situation's bad."

I left Tasha and went to the waterfront.

When I arrived, it was crowded and busy.

Moe helped Ash get organized and Grif and the Bear cabin boys prepared their equipment. Everyone wore life-jackets with the words *Camp Rainbow Wings* written in faded black marker on the back. Choosing the life-jacket seemed to be a big deal. There was lots of play-arguing over the choices.

From personal experience, I knew that some of them stunk. When the campers started to wallop each other with their jackets, Grif had to step in and stop them.

I didn't see Pegasus—the unicorn boat—which was unusual. Usually, it was filled with bouncing kids, screaming and shoving each other into the shallow water near the beach.

When I arrived at the pontoon boat, the kitchen helpers had already loaded it with supplies for the picnic. Cook had carried on big plastic coolers and stacked them at the back.

"Glad you got permission to join us," he said, when he noticed me watching. "The kitchen staff's riding over with me, but there's extra room. Find yourself a life-jacket and take a seat."

At that point, the counselor in the lead canoe blew a horn. The kids in the shore boats hollered, "Ahoy!" and shoved off. I ran over to the beach pole that held the rest of the life-jackets. Moe was there, supervising as Ash climbed into the centre of his canoe and knelt on the bottom boards. When he was inside, Moe clapped his hands.

"ARRRRR! Great job, Ash! I'm going to be right behind you, buddy."

Ash lifted his paddle in the air and held it high over his head. "Treasure Island! ARRRRR!"

Since the nightmare conversation with my parents, I'd avoided being anywhere near Ash. But I'd thought a lot about him. I'd underestimated Ash and wondered how much he knew. Did he know his mom was marrying my dad?

Shielding my eyes from the sun's glare, I watched the campers spread out across the water.

After Moe slid his kayak into the shallow water, I yelled, "Where's Pegasus?"

"The unicorn? It's getting patched again. The plastic's real thin and it tears easy as a piece of paper. Yesterday, the Bear Cabin kids got too rough and ripped a hole in the bottom. Tomorrow, it'll be good to go."

I reached for the last life-jacket left on the pole and plugged my nose. Bleah! The fabric was covered with tiny black spots and smelt mouldy. No wonder the other kids didn't want it. I put it over my shoulders.

"I'll stink if I have to wear this gross thing."

"That's the rule! If you fall in, it could save your life. You better hurry —the pontoon's ready to go." He dug his paddle into the water, and pushed away.

At the dock, there was a steady putter from the pontoon boat's engine. Over on the lake, the kayaks and canoes looked like miniature toys floating in a big bath tub. The paddlers were singing. Words from the campfire sing-a-longs drifted back to the shore.

Ash paddled hard and closed the gap. He joined in the words, adding his own pirate action. "ARRRRR!"

Moe yelled over his shoulder, "Gotta go! See ya on the other side!"

TREASURE ISLAND ADVENTURE

~~~~~~~

Since the disastrous session with my parents, I'd worn a bad mood like a vampire's cloak. However, despite my grouchy outlook, the pontoon boat trip to Treasure Island was a blast. I'd never been on one before. It had a flat bottom and thick cushioned seating around the outside and was sheltered by a multi-coloured striped canopy. It felt as stable on the water as being on the dock.

Cook drove at a slow speed to keep our wake from rocking the little boats, and we stayed away from them.

The pontoon boat was crowded with supplies and people. The other passengers were the same campers I'd been with on the ferry, the first day. At the steering wheel, Bren was beside Cook, learning how to drive. The two kids in wheelchairs were at the back, arguing over which video game was the best. They decided that when camp was finished, they'd meet online and hold a tournament. The guy who wore the helmet, told them 'Anime' was better than any video game. Then he looked at me.

"What do *you* think, Miss Snob?"

What a jerk. That stupid nickname pissed me off. Like me, he'd ignored the 'honest and kind' camp motto. Instead of calling him 'Helmet' or 'Game-boy', I tried to demonstrate that at least *I'd* matured.

"I don't play games . . . uh, sorry, I don't know your name."

"Marsh. I didn't used to be into games either. Until I had to stop hockey and wear this friggin' helmet."

I'd never given Helmet-head any consideration, because I'd decided that he wasn't worth it. Maybe I *had* been a snob. My face burned.

But, under that helmet, he was cute. Dark brown eyes and high cheekbones. Marsh. I repeated his name in my head so I'd remember it.

"Do you always have to wear that helmet, Marsh?"

"Naw. It's because I had a concussion. A few more months and the doctors said I won't need it anymore. But no more high-risk sports. It sucks. I wanted to play in the NHL."

He went back to arguing with the others. I had a feeling that the tiny girl with the baby voice was staring at me, so to avoid her, I turned and watched the paddlers on the water.

"I know who you are." Her voice in my ear was like the dentist's drill. My stomach twisted. Had she been a fan? Was she going to out me in front of everyone?

"You're the girl who dropped her food tray on the floor in the cafeteria. Made a huge mess. Because Grif talked to Willa. You're jealous because you're in love with him."

Her voice was so loud, the entire boat turned and stared.

"She slipped on a wet spot on the floor." Bren spoke up. "You should mind your own business. *You're* the one in love with Grif."

I started to panic. This was too personal. *Don't respond. Divert the attention . . . change the topic.* I waved my hand and pointed at the water.

"I wonder who's going to be first to reach Treasure Island?"

From his position standing at the steering wheel, Cook scanned the water between our pontoon boat and the island. Deep lines formed around his eyes and cheeks as he squinted against the sun.

"Those paddlers have improved since camp started," he said. "When they first started out, they were hopeless. Now, they're much better. Still... even when the water's flat, this is a solid half-hour trip. Keep an eye out. If the waves kick up, it'd be easy for some of them to tip over."

"What would happen? They're wearing lifejackets—" I shaded my eyes to watch.

Cook shrugged. "Dunno. Moe and Grif taught them how to flip the boats and climb back inside. But that's hard ... even for someone who's strong. Some kids had problems even in the shallow water. Out here..." he rubbed his sweaty forehead and sighed.

Everyone heard the tension in Cook's voice and stopped talking.

It was easy to pick out Ash. He paddled solo, singing a pirate song at the top of his lungs. Despite my vow to avoid him, I was amazed.

Head down, pumping his paddle, he'd moved to the head of the group. Most of the other canoes had two paddlers. Managing alone needed extra skill and strength, so Ash's effort stood out. As he dug deep in the waves, the front of his green canoe lifted and fell. It was obvious that he wanted to prove himself.

Cook noticed me staring at Ash. "That kid's phenomenal. Once he listened to Moe's instructions, he took off. He's almost got the strength of a grown man. You know, when he came here, I didn't think he'd last. The change is incredible!"

A few days before, when I'd tried to learn to paddle a kayak, the boat tipped, and I fell—getting in *and* out. My shoulders and arms were still sore. I checked my hands. There was no sign left of the manicure I'd had a few weeks ago. My nails were dirty. A chipped bit of passion-pink nail polish remained on my thumbs. A raw blister was at the base of my fingers.

When the pontoon boat pulled in beside a small dock, the fast paddlers were already at the beach. Grif was waiting there. He waved his arms to direct the landings so nobody crashed.

"Watch out for the submerged logs. Everyone help out." Cook gestured at me and Marsh to move to one side of the boat and Bren went to the other. "This island's never been logged, so the trees are very old here. Some of them break and fall into the lake during wind storms. They're hidden just below the surface. You don't see 'em until you hit 'em."

Our dock was a hundred yards away from the paddlers. While we tied the rope, I recognized a familiar sound. A red squirrel ran along the rocks at the shoreline. It chattered like a grumpy old man.

Get off my property!

We took off our life-jackets and the kitchen helpers unloaded the equipment and food.

Cook pointed at me.

"Raven, catch up with the rest of camp. My team has to get the picnic lunch ready. Go try some of the obstacles. Maybe you'll be the one to find the buried treasure."

He twiddled his moustache and turned back to the boat.

Marsh and Bren had already unloaded most of the gear and there wasn't anything I could do to help.

I was aware of their eyes on me. They had to stay behind because neither of them could do the obstacles. The two kids in the wheelchairs stayed on the pontoon boat and continued to argue about games.

A rough trail led from the beach into the woods. There were shouts and laughter ahead, but I stopped to listen to the sounds of nature before I followed the others. Two birds squawked in the pine trees. Prior to camp, I'd never paid attention to birds. One night, at the campfire program, a local naturalist had talked about identifying wild creatures.

He'd said, "Birds and animals constantly communicate to alert each other, but most humans don't pay attention. Ruffled feathers, perked ears, stamping, hooting, calling ... it's all a way of signaling food or danger. Or attracting a love interest! Listen, and try to guess who's talking, and what they're saying."

I listened.

Nope.

I'd learned to tell a loon from an owl, but couldn't tell the difference between a gull and a raven. Two fighting squirrels burst out of the bushes and chased each other around a tree trunk. Those little dudes were everywhere. They were the paparazzi of the forest, cursing in squirrel language.

I shaded my eyes to gaze at the main campground in the distance. It was the first time I'd been off site since I'd arrived at Rainbow Island. I'd wasted so much time planning an escape. Now that I *was* off Rainbow Island, I wasn't running away... instead, I was going to search for buried treasure.

A long blueish shape stretched across the horizon. The mainland, I guessed. That's where the ticket office for the ferry was; the parking lot where Suzi had left me was behind it. Farther out on the lake, a slow-moving black dot headed towards Rainbow Island. Not a loon. The Poseidon.

In the woods, someone cheered.

I turned and ran towards the noise.

OBSTACLES EVERYWHERE

~~~~~~

When I caught up to the others, they were gathered in a clearing at the base of the first obstacle, where everyone used a metal ladder to climb a gigantic tree. Grif waited to help them at a big wooden platform near the top of the tree. A long, heavy rope dangled through a cut-out section by the edge of the platform. The activity was like something Tarzan would do, a free swing on a rope into the open air. The group of kids at the base shoved and pushed each other while they waited their turn.

Grif helped them buckle into a harness and grab onto the swing rope that was attached to an overhead wire. The wire connected to a tree farther down the hill. One at a time, when the kids were ready, they jumped off the platform and swung into the air.

"Hold on tight," he yelled.

When they flew out into the open space, each one screamed. "ARRRRR!" After a few swings, the rope slowed, and they lowered themselves to the ground. The camper dismounted, and it rolled back to the platform and the next person in line had a turn.

Moe stood at the tree base near a wooden box filled with equipment and gloves, and waved at me to join him.

"You gotta put a helmet on and a pair of leather gloves if you want to do this, Raven." He flapped his arms. "Come on, it's your time to try! This is your opportunity to learn to fly, baby, fly!"

"Your rhymes are worse than ever!" I laughed at him, and my grumpy mood vanished.

"Yeah." He dropped his head and whispered so only I could hear. "I'm tired and it's too hard to maintain. Ash keeps bugging me about it. Do you want a helmet?"

"Thanks, but I'm afraid of heights. I feel dizzy just watching the others."

"No worries. You don't have to do it. They've all got a map to find hidden treasure ..." He rolled his eyes. "First, they have to do every obstacle on the course. All ten of them. Each one is different. It's a circle route that ends here. When they reach the end, there's a fabulous beach picnic. The kitchen staff does an amazing job. Cook's got a fake treasure chest with chocolate coins wrapped in gold foil."

"Sounds like fun."

As the group moved along, I followed at the back. Grif was in the lead, two LITs were in the middle trying to keep control, and Moe brought up the rear with me. Every once in a while, Moe stopped, cupped his ear and peered into the woods like he was looking for trouble.

It bothered me.

"Why do you keep doing that?"

"It's a small island, but you never know. The Owl Lady released lots of injured animals from the sanctuary onto the island. Birds flew over and nested. So keep your eyes open."

The rest of the group was ahead of us, putting on safety equipment for a zip line ride between a pair of giant trees. I heard Ash yell, "Me too!"

Moe lengthened his stride, and I almost had to run to stay with him.

"Are there any bears on the island?"

"Probably not. She brought over birds and small mammals like raccoons or a fox, but there's not enough food here for a big animal to survive." He stopped to catch his breath, and peered into the woods. "But come to think about it—yeah—bears can swim. Maybe once in a while, one comes over here for a visit. Especially if any food is left behind after our picnic."

The sun was relentless. The air was hot and humid, and nasty deer flies swarmed around my head. When the campers finished the zip-line, their clothes were damp with sweat. By then, even Moe was cranky. He swatted at the bugs swarming his head.

"Flies as big as bats ... should have worn a hat."

The treasure hunt continued all morning. The campers climbed trees with cable ladders, swung out on ropes, walked on balance beams, belly crawled over logs and zipped like bees through the trees. I got tired just watching them!

When it was time for a water break, everyone sat in the shade. Some lay on their backs and put hats over their eyes to keep the flies off.

I closed my eyes and my mind wandered.

How had Squeak guessed that I was in love with Grif? I wasn't sure myself. I'd tried to keep our relationship private and had avoided him all morning. When I sat under a pine tree beside Moe, Ash came over and flopped on the ground between us.

Like always, it was impossible to ignore him.

Ash chugged some water, then lay back on the pine needles, arms crossed behind his head. "I'm tired." He closed his eyes and went to sleep.

"That guy ..." Moe leaned back on his elbows. "Man, I'm glad he's asleep. I need a break. Working with him is a big job."

"What are you doing in September?"

"Moving in with my boyfriend. Going back to school. Studying biology."

"*Really*?" I rolled on my side to study him. " I imagined you were a stand-up comedian, waiting to be discovered and be famous. Or maybe an actor. You were forced to work at a kid's camp to pay the rent."

"Wrong." He stretched his arms and cracked his knuckles. "I'm not a typical counsellor – or typical anything. You haven't figured that out yet? Nobody here is. I've been coming here since I was a kid. Always loved JB's clown act and the way he treats people. He lets me fool around with rhymes, but I want to be a doctor. Like Kirra. Maybe a neurosurgeon or a child psychiatrist."

Ash lay stretched out on the ground, between us, mouth open and snoring. A deerfly buzzed around his head and I waved it away.

"You've done an awesome job with Ash."

Hands on his knees, Moe leaned forward and lowered his voice. "In some ways, he reminds me of my little brother who's autistic. Growing up, I've learned a lot. My parents took special training. That's why JB picked me to work with him. It's not easy."

Moe took a long pause, and a drink of water. He slapped a mosquito on his arm and brushed one off Ash's t-shirt.

"Sometimes, I stay awake at night worrying about my brother.

He's a great kid, but non-verbal, and has had setbacks. People can be cruel when they don't understand."

We were both silent. The deerfly buzzed around Ash's open mouth. I flicked my hat and killed it. Moe looked thoughtful. Maybe worried.

"It wouldn't take much to trigger a relapse, and Ash could be in trouble."

"What do you mean? He's doing great."

"I keep a close eye on him and prepare him for things I can anticipate. Loud noises agitate him. He gets anxious. When it gets chaotic, his instinct is to run. He takes stuff literally and mimics the words people say. I can't always predict. No—it wouldn't take much ..."

A lump caught in my throat and I wanted to scratch my arm, but took a deep breath instead.

"Well, why'd you let him go to the Owl Lady's house with me? What if something had happened, and I couldn't help him?"

"He's just a kid, but Raven—in his own way—he loves you. When you're in his vicinity, he watches you, and tries to control his emotions and impulses. He talks about you. He wants to impress you. I've seen how you treat him. He trusts you."

I was pretty sure Moe didn't know about the connection between our parents. The fact that my dad was marrying his mom— that Ash was going to be my stepbrother.

"But you're paid to work after him," I snapped. "I'm not. I can't even take care of myself."

I tried to stand, but Moe grabbed my hand and pulled me back.

"Raven, you're better than that. You hide it, but you have a good heart."

It felt like I'd just been complimented for something I didn't deserve.

Moe kept talking. "His big goal is to show off for his parents. Poor kid ... he wanted the lead in *SHIVERS!* so bad. He doesn't understand. But he has a juggling solo that's amazing. We've practiced with the fire pins."

"Wow." My stomach twisted. I didn't want to think about the last day. I wasn't sure I wanted to see my parents—or Ash's—ever again.

Holding his head between his hands, Moe continued. "For some reason, Ash *hates* Grif. I worry a lot about that. He's memorized Grif's actions and lines in the musical and repeats them. Ash sometimes thinks he *is* a pirate!"

A whistle blew, and the other groups gathered their helmets and gloves for the next obstacle. The sound startled Ash, he jerked and woke up. He jumped to his feet and held his arm out like he had a sword.

"ARRRRR! Avast, you fools! Beware of Captain Calico Jack! No one survives."

"See why I'm concerned?" Moe rubbed his creased forehead. With a light hand, he touched Ash's arm. "It's okay, buddy. Trust me. That's the signal for the other kids. Let's join them. There's only a couple easy ones left to do. At the last one, you can do the Plank Walk challenge. It's the toughie! Raven's gonna watch. Show her you're a brave pirate."

"ARRRRR!" Ash took a pose and pretended to hold off an attacker. "No fear, Lady Ann. Calico Jack will defend you."

Ash and Moe joined up with the others and spent the rest of the morning on the obstacles. I tagged along behind, but as I watched, my mood turned dark.

After all, it was my sixteenth birthday and apparently, not a single person in the entire freaking world cared. Years ago, I'd imagined this day would be special. The TripleT show would hold a big party in a hotel ballroom. There'd be hundreds of guests, celebrities and performers. There'd be champagne. Because it was a special occasion, I'd drink a glass, and have another one—and another one. My parents would be together. They'd offer a toast.

"How wonderful Raven is! The best daughter in the world! Where'd she get her superstar talent? Where'd that amazing voice come from? We don't know, but we're thankful each day that she's our daughter."

In my fantasy, after the dance, someone from TripleT, (the director or producer) would blindfold me and lead me out to the parking lot. There, to gasps of surprise, they'd remove my blindfold and WOW! a beautiful new BMW convertible! FOR ME! The best birthday present ever! Fill in a soundtrack of applause and me singing the song that won me the TripleT championship. My jazzy version of 'Somewhere Over the Rainbow.'

But no. Instead, I was stuck at camp and not a single person had said, 'Happy Birthday.' After the second crappy conversation with my parents, I'd thought a day off would be good. Willa was mad at me about that.

And now, I couldn't do anything because of my fear of heights. Acrophobia, Dr. Hill had called it.

Moe tried to be kind and understanding. Before the end of the course, I was able to watch the kids in the trees, without feeling that I was going to barf or faint. Moe told me to put on gloves and a helmet and hooked me to a harness so I got the feel of it. At the last obstacle, I walked to a tree with him, and tried to climb the rope ladder after Ash went up.

It was the freakin' Plank Walk.

Nope. Not a chance. I put my foot on the bottom rung, climbed two steps and froze. I threw my arms around the tree and squeezed tight. "Help!" Moe had to get me get down.

"It's okay, Raven. You did great, just by going that far. You'll do better next time."

"There isn't going to be a next time," I said when my feet touched the ground.

Then Ash totally flipped out! He'd already climbed the rope ladder—no problem—and started to walk on the planks. They were suspended by ropes to make a bridge between two massive trees. A harness attached to a wire tethered him to an overhead line, so if he slipped, he wouldn't fall to the ground. Far beneath the plank bridge was a deep, dark-blue pond. The proper way to get off, was to take the giant rope swing, and jump when it slowed down, close to the ground.

Even though he was safe, when Ash reached the middle of the obstacle, he lost his courage.

He panicked and sat down, screaming, "Pirates! Jack's going to fall! Crocodiles will kill him!"

Grif went NUTS! Yelled and swore in front of everyone. Called Ash an asshole.

"Get down, you little wimp! I dare you to finish!"

That didn't work. Some kids cried.

Moe ignored Grif and climbed the tree to help Ash calm down, and finish, but for the first time, Moe couldn't.

Ash lay on his stomach, hugging the boards. Moe came back and talked to Grif. After a brief discussion, Grif and Moe climbed up trees from opposite sides, crawled out on the planks and carried Ash, kicking and screaming, back to the starting platform.

He cried, the other kids cried, I cried.

It was awful.

For the rest of the trip, Ash wouldn't talk. He sat by himself on the beach and wouldn't eat lunch. Afterwards, he refused to get into his canoe. Instead, he returned to camp on the pontoon boat. We towed his canoe behind us. He stayed at the opposite end of the boat, curled in a ball, not talking. No one talked. It was horrible.

SWEET SIXTEEN

Things didn't improve after the Treasure Island disaster. It was Indian food night, usually my favourite. The kitchen served butter chicken, vegetarian meatballs, and chickpea curry. But after supper, the Bobcat cabin girls abandoned me in the cafeteria. It was obvious they were trying to avoid me. Throughout the entire meal, they'd shot looks at each other.

I'd made an honest effort to think of their real names, instead of the labels I'd given them. I'd given them honest compliments, in my best 'teen star' voice.

"Lisa, I loved the bracelets you made in Tasha's class today. What a great selection of beads! They turned out amazing!"

"Rhianna, the gymnastics group ... those flips and spins at

the campfire last night. Wow, incredible!"

Tasha seemed shocked, but I was sincere. After the trip to Treasure Island, I was different. Off balance. Disappointed for the kids who couldn't participate. And that included me.

Intrigued by Moe. Mad at Grif. Upset for Ash.

The Bobcat LITs were a private clique that I hadn't even tried to join. But before supper, I vowed to see them differently. Like individuals.

It was too late; like they'd done many times before, they left me alone, with Tasha parked beside me, as usual, fiddling with her food.

Tasha went back to the kitchen for a second helping of fried bananas and rice pudding after they left.

While she was away from the table, I took out a paper napkin and wrote on it:

Bobcat girls:
Rip =Jana (Keeps us organized.)
Squeak=Grace (Kind.)
Spex=Tonda (Best card player)
Stix=Mindy (Puts butter on everything she eats)
Rapunzel/Elsa=Katja (Gymnast)

At the bottom, I added a note: *Try harder to always use their real names. Be decent to them.*

I folded it small and hid it in my pocket to slip into my journal later.

When Tasha returned with her dessert, she said, "It's been a while since we've had a private chat, so let's hang out for a few minutes. How'd you feel about the Treasure Island trip? I heard it turned into a disaster. And that Grif made it worse."

She licked sticky sauce off her middle finger, purposely holding it so I knew what she meant.

I was disturbed by Grif's behaviour but tried to defend him. "He said sorry afterwards. He apologized to everyone for losing his temper. It took both Moe and Grif to carry Ash down the ladder from the Plank Walk. They couldn't even do the Swing Jump. Grif got scratched—"

Tasha interrupted. She pushed back from the table, and glared at me. Little lines had formed around her mouth and her eyes tightened.

"That stupid Plank Walk again! That's where Ravi—the counselor before Grif—fell."

"Nobody ever talks about what happened. Seems suspicious—"

"It was a total disaster. I went to the mainland hospital on my day off, and visited Ravi. He claimed a buddy from the mainland had dared him to have a party. Wouldn't give us a name. When JB and Cook rescued him, they found a cold campfire with broken beer bottles. JB had a temporary rope ladder installed on the tree as a replacement." She shook her head and frowned. "Nothing like that's ever happened before."

My skin prickled. Was Grif involved? *No. He couldn't be.* He was impulsive, not bad. I knocked over my glass and spilled water on the floor. The puddle spread under the table and around Tasha's chair. When I went for a mop, my knees shook. Tasha waited until I'd cleaned up before she said anything else.

"You had another tough conversation with your parents last night, huh?"

Still a mind reader. I nodded. We sat for a moment in silence, then heard a commotion outside the cafeteria. Excited shouting, the sound of JB's ATV, other voices. We went to the door to see what was happening.

In the middle of the field, JB waited in his quad, waving at three people who'd just arrived on the Poseidon. As we watched, he revved the engine and drove to the beach. A cloud of black smoke billowed behind and drifted up to us, which made Tasha cough. JB stopped the quad by the dock and the newcomers climbed inside.

"Who are they?" I glanced at Tasha, who leaned forward, straining to see.

"I dunno. Maybe a medical team ... a lawyer? JB hasn't been in camp much since the last time you and Ash visited the Owl Lady. He's moved in with her. Kirra asked the senior counselors to help run the camp. Moe's leading the campfire program tonight."

She headed towards Bobcat cabin.

"Hurry. We don't want to be late. Let's get warmer clothes. It's getting cooler each night. Summer's almost over."

Summer was almost over. That meant my time at Rainbow Wings would soon end, and I'd have to face Suzi and Jon and whatever dumb plans they'd made for my life.

We went back together to Bobcat cabin, then she stopped at the bottom of the ramp. "I need a moment to tie back this mess. The humidity just wrecks my hair. You go in ahead of me."

The cabin was so quiet, it was eerie. I took the ramp to the porch and opened the door. It was dark inside.

"SURPRISE!"

The lights went on and the Bobcat girls burst out of Tasha's room, waving their arms and screamed, "Happy Sixteenth Birthday, Raven!"

I almost fell over. Multi-coloured streamers hung from the rafters and pink and white balloons were tied to the furniture. The LITs had little paper bags filled with scraps of coloured paper in their hands and threw them in the air like confetti.

An enormous cake, covered with pink icing and sprinkles, sat on the card table in the middle of the room, with sixteen sparklers, ready to be lit. My name was written in white letters on the top. Each of the LITs gave me a birthday card they'd made in the craft class. Wrapped around the neck of a hand-carved wooden loon was a beautiful white and silver beaded necklace and matching bracelet.

It was incredible. And I started to cry.

After we finished eating gigantic slabs of angel-food cake and licked the strawberry buttercream icing from our fingers, Tasha reminded us to grab our red-noses. The LITs pulled noses out of their camp bags and stuck them on their faces, then took turns at the mirror, crossing their eyes and sticking out their tongues. I placed the cards and the loon along the window sill, and put on the bracelet and necklace.

Tasha came over and gave me a hug. "Happy Birthday, Raven. I know a boring camp birthday isn't what you expected. You doing okay?"

I blinked away tears. "Angel food cake. How'd you know that was my favourite?"

"That detail was in the notes your mom sent to Kirra. Bren wanted to make it for you. When you arrived in the kitchen this morning, he was afraid he'd blurt out the secret." Tasha zipped her purple camp hoodie and pulled on a ball cap. "Let's get a move on, Bobcats!"

We were late. The smell of smoke and toasted marshmallows greeted us when we arrived. The campfire was lit and huge flames leapt into the sky. The 'Moose is Loose' rock band pounded out a tune from *SHIVERS!*. It was the song where everyone in the cast pulled out a red-nose and slapped it on their face. The campfire set up was more formal than usual. The tech crew had set up the sound and lighting equipment used for rehearsals and the final production.

The Bobcat girls found an empty bench near the back and we sat close together, our thighs and knees touching. Moe was the MC. Everyone laughed at his jokes and lousy rhymes. When he raised his hand for silence, the senior counselors stood and put their fingers to their lips and shushed the crowd. He grabbed a microphone and waved.

"Raven Lacey, please come to centre stage. This is the day to be proud of your age."

My knees shook and my face burned—partly with embarrassment and partly with something else.

Happiness?

All the way to the fire pit, through the crowd, kids high-fived me. They chanted my name. "Raven! Raven! Raven!"

The band started to play. After the first couple of notes I recognized the tune ... *Happy Birthday*. Moe handed me a huge bouquet of wildflowers.

The crowd sang. They all wore red-noses. Even me.

THE SHOW MUST GO ON

~~~~~~~~~~

Only a few days of camp were left, and time had almost run out to polish *SHIVERS!*. Even though I was a member of the chorus, and not a lead, I'd worked hard in the dance and vocal classes. Because I was older and taller than most, I stayed in the back row. The younger, shorter girls were where I used to be—in the spotlight.

I was okay with it, relieved that the pressure was off.

Every waking minute of camp was spent refining the scenes. Rehearsals, finishing the set, costume fittings, makeup practice, tech rehearsal. I used to work with professionals, but I had to admit—the campers were talented. We moved the dancing and singing onto the stage.

Grif and Tasha had memorized their lines, and they were a

good comic duo. Tasha played the role of Lady Anne, and Grif's character was Calico Jack, a gruff pirate who rescued her from a tiny island, where she tried to survive after a shipwreck. Then a crocodile—Bren, in a wacky green costume with big cardboard teeth—attacked them. Calico Jack got scared and turned into a blubbering wimp and Lady Anne had to save them both.

The script was silly stuff—slapstick humour. When they messed up a line, they improvised, and it was totally hilarious.

It was a bit like my old career, except more fun and less work. Without a big part, I could relax and enjoy myself, and see how all the parts came together.

Before he'd left camp to care for his mother, JB had helped me work on my singing. He'd given me thirty minutes on three afternoons to get my resonators vibrating, and practice singing. I wasn't good. If JB thought he'd work a miracle and fix my voice, he was wrong. He was nice about it, but said performing for an audience would be my choice.

"Relax. Straighten your shoulders, relax your jaw and belly and the sound will come. When you're ready to reach the high notes, you'll feel the good vibrations in your body," he said.

When JB winced at my attempts, it told me all that I needed to know. I wasn't ready to sing in public.

In private, Tasha told me she thought I could do it.

"It's like that 'falling off a horse' expression. Conquer your fear and get back on."

"I can't! I did something so stupid, I ruined my voice. In public. It went viral. People on social media mocked me. Singing in public is asking too much. I can't."

"Think about it. You're different now. Stronger. Happier. Your voice *is* coming back. It's husky, emotional. If you sing at the end of *SHIVERS!*, it'll be a triumphant comeback. Your parents will love it. So will everyone else. Come on, we're a team, and whatever happens, it's always beautiful." Then she laughed. "Well, some years it's a hot mess, and stuff goes sideways. But no matter what, the parents always love it."

In her spare time, when JB wasn't around, Tasha coached me. She was right, my voice *was* different—raspy—but that didn't mean it was good. Because it wasn't. Tasha said I could decide right before the show. They wouldn't put it on the program, so there'd be no pressure. No one would know. If I pulled it off, it would surprise my parents. And maybe they'd forgive me.

I agreed to keep trying.

IT'S OKAY TO CRY

~~~~~~~~~~~~

On the second to last day of camp, Moe stopped the campfire program early. He hadn't been funny all day. It was like his mind was elsewhere. Standing in the centre of the platform, he raised his hand for silence, and the senior counselors and LITs helped settle the campers.

Moe lifted the microphone, lowered his head and struggled to find his words. He was quiet, then he shook his head and began.

"I have something I need to tell you tonight."

"It's your birthday," shouted someone from the Bear Cabin. A few kids laughed.

Moe shook his head and lifted his hand. "No. Something that's hard to say."

That stopped the jokes. The entire camp went dead silent.

"JB called this afternoon with some bad news. He wanted to tell you himself, but he's dealing with a lot of stuff. Some of you already know part of this story. Forty-five years ago, Faena Bean, JB's mother, bought Rainbow Island to establish a wildlife sanctuary. She did good work and saved injured birds and animals. She became famous, and everyone called her the Owl Lady. She never refused a hurt or dying creature. Treated them like her family. JB was raised like that ... seeing the value in each living thing."

He stopped to compose himself.

I glanced around. Everyone was tense, as if they knew that Moe's story didn't have a happy ending. But we didn't know what he'd say.

"The Sanctuary closed ten years ago, and JB's mom has lived alone since then. She wasn't well the last few years, and JB was worried. He hasn't been here lately, because he went to stay with her. To take care of her. Her doctor came and kept her comfortable at the end. JB never left her side. He told me to say that he missed all of you."

I felt cold and shivered. My eyes filled with tears. Beside me, Grace and Jana sniffed.

"This afternoon, at the Sanctuary, JB's mother—the Owl Lady—passed away peacefully. JB was at her side, holding her hand. Before she closed her eyes and took her last breath, he told her that he loved her."

Moe choked and couldn't continue. His shoulders heaved with emotion. He closed his eyes and lowered the microphone. In the pause, Tasha made her way through the crowd over to Moe. She put her hand out to touch him, and whispered something. He nodded, gave her the mic, and stepped away.

"Guys ... it's okay to cry," Tasha said. "It's a sad day. JB wants you to know that his mom is free. There's no more aches and pains. Like the birds she rescued and released, her spirit flew away. She's found her Rainbow Wings."

Tasha's face flushed and her voice broke. Except for the sound of muffled sobs, there was a prolonged silence. She wiped her eyes and resumed. "Tomorrow we'll dedicate our final show to the Owl Lady. I know this is hard. Please take the hand of the person next to you."

She started to sing, 'Lean on Me', a song we sometimes finished the evening with; Moe joined her, then everyone joined in at the first chorus and sang together.

At the end of our bench, Katja and Jana hugged and then the Bobcat girls joined hands. Grace reached for me, and her hand was warm and firm. Tears streamed underneath Tonda's glasses, so Grace handed her a tissue.

My throat tightened, which made it hard to sing. I whispered some of the words and blinked away tears.

Above the voices of the other campers, I heard Ash's voice wail, "Noooooo."

THINKING IT OVER

~~~~~~~~

After the final words, the entire camp was in tears. Many of the kids didn't know the Owl Lady, but because camp was almost over, and they might not see each other afterwards, they were super emotional. After tomorrow, some of the goodbyes might be forever. Moe told everyone to head to the cabins for lights out, and the senior counselor waved flashlights to direct us.

The crowd spread out but didn't move away. Groups formed to hug. Tasha blew JB's horn. "I know it's the final night, but go back to your cabin. No fooling around. Tomorrow's a big day. We put on the parent show, finish packing, and then go home. It's tough, but like the pros say, the show must go on."

As everyone left, I tried to signal to get Grif's attention. The

Bobcat girls held hands, and wandered back to the cabin, and I hung out behind them. Grif found me and we walked together on the path. We didn't talk, it just felt good to have him beside me.

Before we separated, he said, "After they're all asleep, meet me at the waterfront."

I was nervous and confused. Even though I knew about his personal problems, and liked him, some of the stuff he'd done didn't feel right. But JB believed everyone deserved a second chance, and Grif had always apologized for his mistakes.

"Sure."

"Bring your phone." He sounded pissed off.

I wanted to find out how he felt about me. Like Tasha said, tomorrow, we'd all go home. Everyone in Bobcat cabin had started to pack their suitcases to go home.

Would I see Grif when camp was over?

When I got to the cabin, I organized my suitcase. It took a while for the cabin to settle down, but finally, Tasha yelled, "Go to bed, and get to sleep!"

Everyone did.

I lay on my bunk, and waited until there was soft breathing in the cabin. And snoring from Rhen. The LITs were all asleep. The door to Tasha's room was closed. I stripped off my pajamas, put on the camp t-shirt and a pair of navy-blue tights. I didn't bother with underwear. I grabbed my jean jacket off the hook and felt the weight of the phone in the breast pocket.

I tiptoed into the bathroom with my journal, locked the door, and sorted through the photos I'd taken. There were images of the Sanctuary property, the Owl Lady and the campgrounds. When he wasn't looking, I'd even sneaked a few of Ash. I played with the pictures and edited some. Cropped several and changed them into black and white. Even though I'd been in a hurry when

I took them, some of the photos were beautiful.

Would Grif would use them for the photo contest? Would they win? Would that help the camp?

I opened the journal and flipped through the entries. I'd written some mean stuff. I ripped those pages to shreds.

On the last page, I wrote, *Camp's almost over. It wasn't anything like what I expected. But, it was what I really needed.*

Then I went back to the photos on my phone.

As I hurried away from Bobcat cabin, I turned on my phone's flashlight. Grif said he'd charged it for me, but the battery was low.

I was hyper-excited. When I arrived, Grif was there, waiting at the beach. At first, I hoped it would be great—a chance for us to be alone, and talk about our future. But something was wrong. A smell. My skin tingled. Grif had a beer can in his hand and the air around him was sour-sweet.

"Thought you were going to chicken out. Those little brats in my cabin took a long time to settle down. I told them if they moved a muscle out of bed, I'd squash them like a mosquito."

Like it was a joke, he slapped his hand together to prove how he'd crush them, then pointed at the beach. Pegasus had been repaired and re-inflated. It had been pulled up onto the sand, and secured to the lifejacket pole. We took our shoes off, untied the rope, dragged it into the shallow water, and climbed inside.

Grif took a swig from the can, then held it towards me. "Want some?" His face was tight and withdrawn.

I hesitated.

"Come on. It's the last night of camp. It's a tradition for the counsellors to party."

"I don't drink."

"I dare you." He held it out to me.

I wanted to say no. But despite everything that had happened,

I wanted him to like me. I took the can, and took a deep gulp to show I wasn't afraid. It was awful. Burned my lips and tightened my throat. I wasn't used to drinking. When Suzi managed my career, she'd kept me in bubble wrap. I wanted to spit it out.

"More?"

"Sure." I took another gulp and faked a smile. "Can we talk about the future?"

"It happens. What about it?" He shrugged and passed me the can.

I felt woozy and knew I shouldn't have any more, but I took another big drink. "I mean ours. Our future. When camp's over, how will I find you? Maybe I could go with you ... when you go to college. You said your dad would pay your way."

"If I ruined the camp and forced the old lady and JB to sell out." *There it was. The truth.*

My stomach lurched, and I shook my head to clear it. It took me a few seconds to process his words.

He wasn't sorry about anything. He'd used me.

"The Owl Lady died ...," My words stumbled over each other.

"And left her estate and property to JB. She lived like a goddamn pauper, but she had enough money invested to keep the camp going for a long time. I need the photos you took to show what a dump the place is. If they're bad enough, it might make a difference. We could use them to force JB out. Give me your phone." He pushed my shoulder. "Now."

I pulled back.

He took another drink. I slapped his hand, and beer spilled on my legs and puddled on the bottom of the boat.

"Bitch! After all I've done for you. I said, *give me* the phone."

"No! Rainbow Island is beautiful. I don't want it sold to a developer and turned into a theme park. It would ruin everything."

"You're a fool, Raven. Tomorrow morning, I'm outta here. I got fired! In the morning, before breakfast, Dad's sending a boat over to get me. Somehow, that dumb-ass JB learned who my father is. And he figured out that I dared Ravi to go on the plank walk that night. How else could I get a job here?"

He punched his fist against an open palm. "Someone ratted about how I feel about the campers. Most of them are little jerks. It's a total waste to send them here. Especially that nut that's got a crush on you. What's his name? Ass? Give me the phone."

"You creep! His *name* is Ash. And he's a million times better than you! Every *single* person here is better than you are. Forget about my phone, Grif. There's *nothing* on it. I had a bad feeling about your so-called photography contest . . . and before I came here tonight, I deleted everything."

"Wha—!" He stepped over the unicorn's wing, tripped and fell to his hands and knees. He used a string of profanity worse than I'd ever heard before.

My horrible, uncontrollable inner monster woke up. I felt it arrive. It was the same feeling as the night of the TripleT disaster. I hadn't swallowed poison, but my body felt like I had. I fell to my knees.

He held up his phone.

"I'm gonna wreck you, Raven."

"No! Please don't do this ... *please.*"

He belched. Then he shook his head and laughed. His grin was grotesque, one side of his mouth drooped and twisted. His eyes gleamed. He was the nightmare clown I'd dreamed about.

"You're pathetic. Don't kid yourself anymore. Before that show, you were never close to being famous. Until the last episode, no one gave a damn about you. At least a hundred times, I've watched the video of your breakdown. I even shared it again when

I got here. Hilarious. I'm filming right now ... you on your knees ... begging at my feet. And I'm gonna share it with the world. You're a total disaster. See ya, *loser.*" Then he laughed, and shoved the phone in his pocket.

He turned, and started to walk away, but tripped again on a paddle that had been left lying on the beach. Swearing, he floundered a few steps in the soft sand, flung his arms out, and twisted his body to maintain his balance. He stopped long enough to hurl another curse at me, then stood upright, and walked away.

I curled in a ball and sobbed. Rocked. Pounded my fist. My vision spun.

I was lost. Lost. Lost.

Then it all went black. Just like six months before, behind the stage curtain, I passed out.

CALICO JACK GOES TO SEA

~~~~~~~~~

It was dark. I blinked and squinted at the night sky, trying to figure out what was happening. The unicorn boat bounced on the waves, while I lay on my back and gazed at the stars. Where was I? What time was it?

Nothing made any sense. It seemed hours since I snuck out of Bobcat cabin. One thing was clear, though. I'd made a total fool of myself. *Grif.* I tried to get the image of his ugly, twisted face out of my head. Just thinking about him made my face burn. What if he *had* filmed me on my knees, drunk? Was I going to be publicly shamed again? I felt sick. And not just from the alcohol.

I propped myself on an elbow, rolled over and got to my

knees. A terrible thing was going to happen, I felt it. I was in deep trouble. Somehow, Pegasus had floated into the middle of the lake. Just like I'd warned Suzi and Kirra I would two weeks ago, I was leaving camp. I'd run away.

My skin prickled when I realized that I wasn't alone—someone else, very near me, was panting. I heard a splash. Pegasus lurched and swayed as the person—I didn't know who—mumbled words I couldn't understand. I squinted and made out a dark figure, standing by the unicorn's neck, swinging a kayak paddle.

It was Ash.

My stomach tightened. I lifted my head and peeked over the unicorn's side.

It was bad.

We were way outside the camp area, far from the shore. I was so scared, I couldn't move. Then I heard voices--my dad, my therapist, JB and Tasha—all in my head at once.

Focus! Assess. Control your response. Think! I realized that if I screamed, it would get much, much worse. I took a deep breath and tried to keep my voice calm and controlled.

"Ash ... what's going on? We're supposed to be asleep in our cabins. Why are we out here on the lake?"

When he answered, his voice was gruff, like he was pretending to be older. He lifted his chin. "Not Ash... I'm Calico Jack, the famous pirate!"

Oh no, I thought. That was Grif's introductory line in the *SHIVERS!* production. I tried not to panic. *Think! Think! Think!*

Ash leaned against the unicorn's neck and peered into the water. It was pitch-black.

"Crocs are in there... ARRRRRR!" He raised his arm over his head and flung a small object into the water. I heard a splash.

"Choke on it," he yelled.

Tension, I thought. *Get rid of it.* I counted to ten. *Breathe in ... out ...in ... out. Relax your shoulders. Breathe.* For the first time ever, I hoped it would work.

"Ash, listen to me. We don't have life-jackets on. We need to turn Pegasus around and go back to the beach. I don't know if you passed the swim test, but I barely did."

"Pirates don't take tests!" He crossed his arms on his chest. What he said next was a wild mix of Grif's lines in the play, plus his own ideas.

"Lady Anne, I heard crying. And that asshole Grif! I kidnapped you. You're my captive. Watch the harbour. They won't take us alive. We'll fight the scurvy dogs, slit their throats and throw their guts in the sea!" He waved a long knife over his head.

"Where'd you get that knife, Ash? Put it away before someone gets hurt."

"A sword! From the mess hall. It's mine!"

That didn't make sense.

"Ash, what are you talking about?" He didn't answer, but I figured it out. After supper, while his cabin mates cleaned the cafeteria, he must have taken a carving knife from the kitchen.

He pointed at me. "Maintain a sharp lookout. We'll *die* before anyone takes us back."

The wind pushed us farther out, waves splashed against Pegasus's wings, and it tipped sideways. I clenched my hands and swore. My mind raced, trying to remember how Moe had de-escalated Ash in previous episodes.

Keep calm, I told myself. *Keep calm!*

"Ash, it's past midnight—we're not in a pirate ship. This is Pegasus. It's supposed to stay near the beach, not out in deep water. The pirate play isn't real; we've been pretending. Ash, I don't want to be a pirate anymore."

He hung his head and hunched his shoulders, so I hoped he was listening.

"When the sun comes up, everyone finishes packing their bags to go home. Your mom and Jon will come soon—they'll be worried if you're not there. Ash, let's turn Pegasus around and head back to the beach."

"NOT ASH! NOT PRETENDING! I'M JACK!" He yanked his camp shirt off and pointed his knife at something ahead in the dark. "ONWARD!"

He was having a full out meltdown. Far worse than anything I'd ever seen at camp. I watched the distant lights of Rainbow Wings and mumbled a prayer. There had to be a way to help him. So much could go wrong, and we could both end up dead. He raised his arm and increased the volume of his voice.

"Stay with me, Lady Anne! We'll sail the Seven Seas seeking treasure." He pointed forward, and moonlight glittered on the beaded bracelet on his wrist. He'd made it in Tasha's craft class. It was like the one the Bobcat girls had given me.

"Ahoy! Land ahead. Prepare to disembark!"

As we neared the shore, he recited more lines from the play, then waved his knife at me to follow him. Right before we landed, Pegasus's plastic bottom made a scrunchy, ripping sound. My skin prickled. I remembered Cook's words. *More trouble.* We'd scraped over a submerged log just off Treasure Island. Trying to keep my balance, I staggered to my feet. Ash scrambled out to the beach, patted the unicorn's horn, then jammed his knife blade into a tree trunk.

"I claim this land for Calico Jack and Lady Anne." He yanked the knife out, tucked it back into his belt, and ran along the rocks on the shore's edge. It was like he'd turned into an angry red squirrel, the one that cursed at me.

I climbed out over the rainbow wing, into the shallow water and waded to the shore. My tights were soaked, and my feet burned with cold, but I followed him. It was hard to remember to stay calm. Instead, I screamed.

"Ash, where the hell are you going?" So much for staying calm.

"Find buried treasure!" He waved a piece of paper. "With William Kidd's map."

"No! That's the Rainbow Wings Camp brochure. We came here for the obstacle course, and the *treasure* was our lunch! I told you—we shouldn't be here at night. It's not safe. I'll signal so the camp can help us." I turned on my phone's flashlight.

"No signals!" He snatched the phone out of my hand, and tossed it into the lake. "Have to hide! If they capture us, they'll sentence me to death."

I grabbed his arm, but he shoved me aside. "They'll never take me alive!" Then he turned and fled into the woods.

I splashed into the lake to search for my phone. Near the boat I stepped on something hard. I yanked my phone out of the water, wiped it dry with my shirt and tried to turn it on.

Nothing.

When I leaned against Pegasus, it collapsed like a punctured balloon. The bottom had torn when we landed.

Telling myself *don't freak out*, but freaking out anyway, I went to the path between the pine trees.

"Ash ... where are you? We have a problem ... we're stuck here!"

No answer. My voice got louder.

Crash! A whimper in the bushes ahead caught my attention. I ran towards the noise, yelping when sharp twigs and pinecones crunched under my bare feet.

"Ash! Wait for me!" Whip-like branches slapped my face. I tripped over a tree root and sprawled on the ground. My knees hurt, my hands hurt, but I got to my feet, and screamed for him. "Ash? Answer me!"

"Help! Jack is trapped!" His voice came from somewhere ahead, high in the trees. He sounded terrified.

I staggered to my feet and followed the noise. The path led into a large cleared area I remembered from the treasure hunt. He'd reached the obstacle course. There was enough moonlight to see the beams, bridges, nets, zip line, and water pit. But no sign of Ash.

I closed my eyes and listened. Then I heard him scream, "Crocodiles!"

"Calm down, Ash! I'm coming to help. Tell me where you are!"

"Here! Where he tried to make Ash walk the plank."

A sharp pain stabbed in my chest. That's where he'd had the meltdown during the Treasure Hunt. That time, it took both Grif and Moe to carry him down.

I heard Dr. Hill's words, *"Assess the situation."*

I squinted into the sky, straining to see. It was impossible. When I saw the obstacle, my stomach twisted.

It was just like I remembered it. Suspended high above a pond, the Plank Walk dangled between two gigantic hemlock trees. When we'd been there before, at both ends there'd been ladders that led to two elevated wood platforms high up in the trees. The Jump Swing that he didn't do last time, was the proper way down from the last platform. It was hard to do in the daylight with an instructor and safety equipment, and unthinkable in the dark.

I stood at the bottom of one of the trees, and called to him, trying to control my tone.

"Ash ... do you have on a harness and a helmet?"

Focus! Stay in control. Keep calm.

When he answered, he sounded as scared as I was.

"NOT ASH! Pirates don't wear helmets!"

Then I saw him, high overhead. He lay on a skinny board, half-way across the suspended wood planks. His body was curled into a ball, rocking.

My jaw tightened. A big lump jammed my throat, and I had to swallow it to talk. "Okay. Stay there and I'll climb up to you."

"No ladder."

My stomach twisted. "What do you mean, no ladder?"

"The crocodile ate it."

I groped around the trunk trying to find the rope ladder. Blobs of sap and rough bark scratched my hands. My foot caught in a jumble of ropes and metal rungs, and I tripped and fell. I lay flat out in the pine needles, trying to think. When I stretched out my arms, my fingers touched the cut end of a rope.

It hadn't been eaten by a crocodile. Ash had climbed partway up the ladder, then used his knife to slice the rope and let it all drop to the ground.

It was impossible to follow him from here.

I wanted to run away—signal a passing boat—get off the island. Let him stay there.

But I didn't.

"Ash, hang on. I'm going to the other end. Don't be afraid and don't let go!"

Overhead, the plank bridge creaked and swayed in the breeze.

"Pirates have no fear—" He broke off sobbing. "The crocodiles are coming ..."

It was almost morning, but wisps of fog lifted from the forest floor, and made it harder to see. I groped my way to the tall tree that marked the opposite end of the obstacle. At the base of the tree was a storage box where the counselors had dumped the heavy leather gloves everyone wore for protection.

After I tied a pair of gloves into my t-shirt, I shoved my hands into another pair. Then I grabbed the ladder and nudged my bare foot around until my big toe stubbed against a metal tread.

I froze. My heart banged against my ribcage.

What if I had a panic attack? He was so high! My knees knocked together. I took a deep breath and counted to ten. I had to conquer my phobia of heights. I had to climb. I had to save Ash.

I held my breath, tugged the ladder straight, leaned back and scrambled up the rungs. Just as I grabbed the edge of the platform, my foot slipped. A bolt that held the ladder to the tree popped out, and one side of the ladder fell away. I threw myself flat on my stomach onto the platform.

When I caught my breath, I crawled to the edge and peeked over. The ladder dangled loose. We wouldn't be able to use it to get down. The only option we had was to use the Jump Swing and lower ourselves down. I didn't know whether to swear or cry, so I did both.

Ash heard me and screamed, "They'll kill me!" He yelled it over and over.

I pulled myself together. *Think!*

I crawled to the edge of the platform where I could see him. "Ash, I'm at the finish—just in front of you. I can't reach you, so you have to stand up and walk the plank. You can do it. Then we'll get down and go back to Pegasus."

"Ash couldn't do it. He failed the course. The crocodiles ate him."

He didn't budge.

Whoever he was ... Ash or Calico Jack, I wanted to leave him right there. To get to the ground before I passed out. To run away.

But I couldn't. I needed to make a connection with him. To help him.

"Listen Ash, when you fail ... you try again. Just like me. I know you can do it."

He lifted his head and stared at me.

"Ash, you're brave ... you're strong. Come on ... I'm waiting for you."

Slowly he uncurled, then stood, hunched and tottering until he found stability on the plank. He took a step. The bridge creaked and swung, tilting side to side. His arms flailed, and he struggled to find his balance. He put a foot down fast and hard, the bridge lurched, and he slipped and fell. One leg slid between the boards and he collapsed onto his stomach.

"Ash died! Crocodiles chewed off his legs."

I thought my heart would burst out of my chest. I felt dizzy and was afraid to look at him. He whimpered, so I tried again.

"Ash, trust me. Don't quit because you had trouble with this before. There aren't any crocodiles here. You *can* do this. You're brave! But I'm stuck. I need your help to get off with the Swing."

I gulped and continued. "When I count to three, pull on that line and reach for the ropes running along the sides. When you stand up, take giant steps between the boards. Go slow. Hold on tight to the cables. Ash ... are you listening?"

His voice was small. "Yes."

"You're going to be okay. Now ... one ... two ... three—"

He yanked himself upright, and took a cautious step forward to the next plank.

"Fantastic! I'll count and you keep doing that." The bridge swayed, but Ash clung to the ropes and took another step. One at a time, he did it, and made it safely across the obstacle.

When he stumbled onto the platform deck, I hugged him. He squeezed back, hard. I felt the throb of his racing heart against mine. We sat together on the platform, almost hysterical. Both of us laughed and cried at the same time. An owl was hooting nearby when we calmed down enough to hear it.

Ash got upset again.

"The Owl Lady—she's gone! I miss her." He wailed and banged his head on the ground. It scared me, but I threw my arms around him and held him so tight, I felt his ribs. He relaxed and made eye contact.

"Sing for me, Raven."

"What are you talking about? We're stuck in a tree and it's not even daylight. I can't sing here."

"The Blackbird song . . . for me. Sing, Raven."

I didn't want to sing—it was a stupid place and a stupid time. No adoring crowd, no agents lined up to offer me a contract, no cash prizes to be won. My voice had been ruined. I didn't want to sing.

"Sing, Raven." He put his head on my shoulder, relaxed and closed his eyes.

I began to sing.

Rocking him like a baby, I sang the song the Owl Lady had taught us. About broken wings and flying away. About being free. He hummed with me and joined the chorus. We were two people in a dangerous place, singing a duet. Unreal.

I had a weird premonition. Soon, we were going to be step-siblings. In some safe place, with the new baby we were going to share, we'd sing together again. Maybe.

For the first time since the 'incident', my voice was clean and pure. Almost like it used to be when I was a little girl all by myself, just singing because I loved it; it was perfect—maybe even better. It felt right. Was it good enough to win the TripleT show?

No way.

I'd need more practice, more training to ever be at a professional level. But just maybe—I could try again, someday. On my own terms. If we ever got home.

MY NEW BFF

~~~~~~~~~~

At last, it was dawn. The owl hooted again, little hoots. Over and over. Above the trees, a soft grey light glowed. I hugged Ash.

"That was amazing! Listen to the owl cheering! Maybe it's Blackbeard. I'm so proud of you."

"I'm Ash. You're Raven." He stared, wide-eyed. "You're happy now. Why were you crying before?"

I leaned against him and squeezed his hand. "Because someone broke my heart."

"You mean Grif. I hate him. Fed his treasure to the crocs." He stroked my cheek. "You're pretty, Raven. Now I'm your boyfriend."

My cheeks burned, and I blinked. "His treasure?"

"His phone. I found it in the sand by Pegasus. Threw it away."

I was stunned. Ash *had* thrown something into the lake! He'd found Grif's phone! He must have dropped it when he tripped on the paddle. There were no photos to worry about!

"You're a great guy, Ash. My BFF."

He sighed and laid his head on my shoulder. "We stay at Rainbow Wings. Forever."

The woods were full of sounds, as we leaned shoulder-to-shoulder; a woodpecker knocked on a tree, and a loon called on the lake. The sun was high enough that light flickered low through the pine trees. It was around 6:30 AM, I guessed.

"Summer's over, Ash. Camp's finished and we'll all leave soon. You're going home with your mom and Jon."

He shook his head. "No! They're mean! Forcing me to go to a different school. Don't want to—" His bottom lip trembled, and his nose dripped. "Want to stay! I'm scared, Raven."

I dropped my gloves, untied the knot in my shirt and handed him the extra pair. "I know. Me too. But we have to go. Ash, your mom and Jon picked a special place, because they want to *help* you. They're good people. It'll be hard at first, but it'll get better. You and I are both going to start over. We'll be a family."

I waited as he put on the gloves, then pointed to the opposite side of our platform.

"To get down, we have to do the Jump Swing. Without the safety harness. It'll be scary, but you're brave. Hold on and swing out from the big tree, then lower yourself to the ground when it slows down. When you're at the bottom, I'll follow. Ready?"

He nodded, kissed my cheek, and ran for a thick rope that dangled from a metal guy wire attached to the platform's edge.

"Hey—go slow! Take it easy or you're gonna get hurt." I ran after him but wasn't fast enough. He grabbed the rope and jumped off the platform. The cable spun out and like a monkey on a vine, he flew through the air. When it slowed, he lowered himself, half gripping, half sliding. At the ground he let go.

The rope bounded back to the edge of the platform.

"Yahoo! He did it! Ash passed the test! He didn't need help!" Ash danced in a circle and pumped his fists. "Your turn, Raven!"

Relieved, I searched for my leather gloves. I found one. Where was the other? Heart pounding, I checked the entire platform. Useless. Nothing. I squatted and looked over the edge.

Whoa... It made me so dizzy I thought I was going to faint. I'd forgotten how high we were.

Don't panic! I slowed my breathing and tried again.

"Oh, no..."

My lost glove was down on the ground. Ash stood beside it and held his knife in the air.

"He's free! Ash not going back—" His words trailed off, and he whooped and disappeared into the woods.

I had no choice.

On my knees, I mumbled a prayer to whoever would help me – god or goddess or crabby squirrel—and slipped the remaining glove onto my right hand. I straightened, counted to three, reached for the rope and leapt into the air.

Whoosh—my heart flipped when I stepped off the platform into nothing. I gulped and held tight, stomach lurching as the cable whizzed away from the tree.

Like a pendulum, I swung back and forth, back and forth. It felt sickening. Then gradually, the movement slowed until the rope came to a standstill. I wrapped my legs tight and dangled. Then I stretched my gloved hand as far as I could, grabbed the rope and squeezed.

I lowered my bare hand ... and plummeted.

My bare hand scraped against the rope fiber. It felt like my skin was being ripped off. In spite of the pain, I tried to hold on. My gloved hand slipped, and the rope ripped and burned through my tights and my t-shirt. Twisting, kicking, pulling ... nothing helped. I slid down the line, feeling it tear my clothes, my legs, my hands, the pain biting like a knife as it sliced through my skin.

My feet smashed on the ground, and the force threw me onto my back. And everything stopped.

CALL MY NAME

~~~~~~~~~~

Someone called my name and shook my shoulders. I opened my eyes. The sight made me feel sick. The sky, the trees, the rocks in my line of vision rocked back and forth, but close to my nose was a familiar face, calling my name. I whispered to him.

"Ash."

He knelt beside me and stroked my arm.

"Pegasus is dead. Flat as a pancake. No escape."

"Ash—I'm hurt."

"Are you pretending? Raven, are you dying?"

I groaned, tried to sit, and collapsed. There was too much pain.

"Pegasus will be fine. He just needs a patch. I'm not dying, but I'm hurt bad. Run and get help."

He hesitated and turned his head away. "Can't. They'll take you away and send me to jail."

The bushes rustled. We both held our breath. Nearby in the woods, branches cracked and snapped as a large animal approached. My vision was dim and blurry, but I heard heavy breathing and a snort. And another snort. More leaves and branches snapped.

They were the noises a bear would make.

I tried again to move and couldn't. Ash's eyes widened, and his jaw dropped.

"The croc! It's coming ..."

Ash leapt to his feet, waved his knife and yelled, "Scurvy dog! I'm ready... fight to the death!" He slashed at the branches. The snorts stopped and Ash yelled again.

"Keep away! Or you'll walk the plank!"

Whatever it was hesitated, then huffed and ran in the opposite direction until we couldn't hear it any more.

Ash threw his head back and yelled, "ARRRRR!"

I moaned and closed my eyes. From far away, I heard Ash call my name, but I couldn't answer. I wondered if I was paralyzed.

Was I having a heart attack?

Was I dying? My eyes flickered open.

He rocked back on his heels, then raised his arm and counted.

"One ... two ... three!" He yanked off his beaded bracelet, and slid it up my wrist. "Protection from the crocs." He pressed my hand to his lips. "My Lady Anne." Raising his chin, he thrust out his chest and held his blade aloft. "Onward!"

My eyes closed. My consciousness drifted as waves of pain washed over me. My side and legs felt like they were on fire. It seemed like a dream, a painful one. One where I might not wake up.

I didn't see him race along the path, then stand beside the flat plastic mess that had been Pegasus, wave his shirt, and signal the camp. But he must have, because through the blackness and suffering that swallowed me bit by bit, I heard him scream.

"HEY! ANYONE ... MY NAME IS ASH AND WE NEED HELP!"

BROKEN WINGS

~~~~~~~~~

It smelled like cleaning supplies. Equipment beeped. Even with my eyes shut, it was bright. My arm hurt. When I opened my eyes, it was noisy, and a blurry crowd of people stood around my bed. Someone shrieked, "She's awake!" and I recognized Suzi's voice. The mouths on the faces all reacted; wide open, smiles, words spilling out in a jumble of sounds.

"Where am I?" It was totally confusing. I lifted my hand and saw a big bandage attached to my wrist. From the bandage, a plastic tube connected to a bag that dangled over my head. A white cast covered the other arm. "What day is it?"

As she leaned her forehead against mine, tears ran down Suzi's cheeks. "You scared the life out of us—the doctor says you were

234

lucky—you're going to be okay, sweetheart." Her face crumpled, and she put a tissue to her eyes and stepped back.

Jon's eyes and nose came into view and he kissed my cheek.

"You're in the North Superior Hospital. You've been unconscious They brought you here two days ago in a helicopter. But you're going to be okay now. It's all going to be okay."

"Thanks, Jon."

"Please call me Dad." He turned to Suzi and she nodded. "No more of that first name stuff. We're your parents—your mother and father. For a while, we were terrified we were going to lose you. We've talked this over. From now on, it's Mom and Dad."

Suzi's head appeared beside his. "We're not getting back together, but we're gonna try to be better parents. Okay?"

"Wha—?" I couldn't move. My leg was in a plaster cast, suspended from a rope that went to the ceiling. "Hey—what's wrong with me? What happened?"

"Let me tell!" I recognized Ash's high pitched voice. "You fell, Raven! Broken bones!"

My vision cleared, and I recognized the faces of the other people standing around the bed. Besides my parents and Ash, JB and Kirra were there. After my parents kissed and hugged me, they stepped back, and let JB come closer. He still wore his tie-dye camp shirt and held his green bowler in his hand.

When his grizzled face came close, I felt my face burn with shame. If I wasn't stuck in a hospital bed with a broken leg, I'd run away to avoid him. I knew our conversation wouldn't be easy. He probably hated me for running away with Ash, wrecking Pegasus and then destroying the last day and *SHIVERS!* Another complete disaster to add to my record.

Before he spoke, I blurted, "I'm really, really sorry, JB. I made a mess of everything—I didn't mean for this to happen." My throat closed and I choked. "I made some terrible choices. I love Rainbow Wings—" Tears filled my eyes and I couldn't say another word.

He squeezed my hand. This time, no clown buzzer.

"It's okay, Earth-child. I'm not mad. I'm just relieved that Ash got our attention, and we were able to get you to the hospital."

I whispered so only he could hear. "What about the show? Was it ruined?" I wanted to ask about Grif, but at the same time, I never wanted to hear his name again.

Somehow, JB knew what I needed.

"For a while there, it was chaos! Before breakfast, Grif's dad sent over a boat to get him." JB's face tightened and he stopped talking.

Kirra took over. "Raven, when we hired Grif, we had no idea what he was like. His attitude and behaviour went against *everything* that's important at our camp. We hope he gets help and straightens himself out."

Suddenly, Ash yelled, "Make that scurvy dog walk the plank! Feed him to the crocs!" Even though everyone was trying to be polite, Ash's words were exactly what I was thinking. I was glad he said it out loud. I burst out laughing and instantly regretted it.

It hurt!

Ash had more secrets to blurt out.

"Calico Jack walked the plank. Lady Anne sang to him."

"Wha—?" Jon—Dad was confused. "Ash, what are you talking about?"

"The obstacle course . . . Ash did the plank walk. I was with him," I said.

"Wha—?" It was JB's turn to be confused. "Is that why you were on the island? Is that why you fell out of that tree?"

"Lady Anne saved Calico Jack! She saved him from the crocodile." Ash's face brightened, and he threw his arms up. "No,

236

no. Ash is pretending. He ran away. Raven saved him." Ash stared at Jon. "I love Raven. She sings like a bird." He flapped his arms. "Like the Owl Lady showed us."

When I found my voice, it came out louder than I intended.

"Grif dared Ash to do the Plank Walk, and humiliated him when he couldn't. Ash tried to prove he could do it."

Someone sniffed, and everyone wiped their eyes.

"I love you, too, Ash." But I was still worried. "What happened afterwards, JB? What about the show—?"

JB rubbed a hand through his hair. "Moe and Tasha were frantic when they discovered the two of you were missing. Tasha came to the office and contacted us, while Moe went down to the beach. He heard Ash scream for help and took the boat over. Moe found you unconscious on the ground and started First Aid."

JB's eyes met the worried gaze of my parents. Mom grabbed my hand as he continued.

"After the helicopter left, we held a meeting with the counsellors and campers. When we learned you were going to be okay, they wanted to go on with the show. Ash was exhausted, but frantic. Because he'd memorized Grif's lines, Moe let him play the lead to help him calm down. It was a good idea. Tasha was fine with it and played along." JB smiled at Ash. "You did great!"

JB winked and leaned in closer, so only I could hear.

"He got carried away with some of the lines and actions. But Tasha improvised. It was terrific."

"JB, I'm sorry about so much . . . and about your mother—the Owl Lady."

There were tears in JB's eyes. "I'm glad you met her. She was pretty darn special. We had some hard times. I messed up, but she forgave me. In a way, you helped us reconnect. I'll always miss her—"

"Blackbird! JB sang it!" Ash interrupted him.

"Wha—?" I tried to prop myself on an elbow, and the pain in my side made me fall back on the bed. Suzi—Mom gasped and squeezed my hand. Dad put his arm around Ash's shoulder, and continued the conversation when Mom moved away.

"Your mother stayed in the hospital. After I checked on you, I went back to the camp to see Ash and get all the gear."

He held up my journal. "Found this under your bed. I didn't peek, but seems like you used it."

"Thanks, it helped. How'd you like the show?"

"Mia and I watched, and we loved it. Great set, singing, dancing . . . the kids who performed were all incredible. Funny too. Tasha—what an amazing talent! At the end, JB sang an old Beatles song, as a tribute to his mother."

JB and Kirra glanced at each other, and Kirra signaled towards the hospital room door, where a nurse talked quietly to Suzi—Mom. JB put on his green bowler and adjusted the angle.

"Okay, Earth Child . . . we'll head back to the island." He gestured towards a pile of flowers and cards on a side table. "There's lots of goodies there for you. All the campers have gone home, but there's stuff back at the island that we have to take care of."

"Will you have to sell the camp?" JB and Kirra had reached at the door, so I yelled, and it came out louder than I expected. Every person in the room froze.

JB turned around. His mouth opened and closed. Kirra took his hand, then leaned her head against his shoulder.

"There's a lot going on right now," she said. "Raven, everyone sends you love and best wishes for a speedy recovery. Read the messages in the cards. Keep in touch, and let us know how you're doing."

THE SOUND OF A RAINBOW

~~~~~~

It was early morning in late October. Overnight, there'd been a rainstorm, with a long period of lightning and explosive thunder. It had been unusually hot, but the air had turned cool and fresh. At breakfast, my mother, the former popstar-turned-talent-recruiter, who now worked in a women's clothing store, opened the mail, as I finished eating a slice of toasted sourdough bread slathered with homemade peach jam.

My phone was propped up against the peanut butter jar, and I scrolled through my social media accounts while she got ready to leave for work. In thirty minutes, the school's mini-bus that was equipped for wheelchairs would arrive. In a week, when I'd be able to walk more confidently, I could take a regular bus. I couldn't wait.

"Mom, listen to this—Wednesday, the Bobcat girls are having an on-line party to celebrate Jana's birthday. The whole cabin's getting together. What should I wear—"

She interrupted me. "I got a message from your doctor. Now that your casts are off, they're scheduling physio appointments."

"Tomorrow after school, I need to shop for the new baby. Friday night, they're having a baby shower. I need a present for Ash, too. Hope he won't be jealous and have a setback after the baby arrives. Dad says the new school's helping him a lot."

"Raven—are you listening to me? You start tomorrow and go twice a week."

I glanced up from my phone. Mom held a brochure from a physiotherapist's office in her hand.

"Don't give me that face." She wagged a manicured finger. "It's a great opportunity, and we're lucky to get you registered. Your doctor recommended it, and your father and I agreed. The clinic has a hot tub and a swimming pool."

"Don't *my* plans count? I'm sixteen, not a kid. I've got stuff after school . . . School Council and Choir practice. I don't want to go."

Mom's phone vibrated. The corner of her eye twitched.

"You're right." She ignored the phone. "You're not a little girl. And I'm not your manager—I'm your mother. Physio will help. Whenever you're ready, you can schedule your own appointments."

I nodded and scrolled through my messages. There were lots of updates. Moe was at med school, Tasha had designed a gorgeous black and gold beaded necklace, and sold it to an influencer. My father had posted a picture of Mia and Ash on the front steps of their new house. Mia was very pregnant.

"Something special came in the mail for you," Mom said.

"Dad says they've finished painting my bedroom, but Mia

wants me to pick out curtains. They forwarded a link...oh cool..."

"I put the physio brochure on the table. Read it when you can tear yourself away from that thing. How'd you manage at camp without it?"

My phone pinged, but I ignored it and met her eyes. "Camp was great, but that part sucked."

Mom headed for the door. "I might be late tonight; the store manager wants a meeting over a new line of accessories. Made from recycled materials. It could mean a promotion." She checked her hair in the hall mirror. "This lipstick doesn't match my dress. I'll have to change."

Some things never change.

I glanced through the mail she'd left. At the top of the pile was a familiar flyer, updated for next summer. On the front cover was a close-up photo of a red-nosed clown, with a tie-dye shirt and a bowler hat. In the sky, Pegasus flew over a rainbow. Duh. I laughed. What took me so long to see the connection between that image and the boat that Ash and I ran away in?

I flipped through the information. Familiar, familiar...new.

This year, Rainbow Wings nature program expands to include the Faena Bean Wildlife rehabilitation complex, situated on the grounds of a former animal sanctuary. This new facility is thanks to an endowment fund from the 'Owl Lady' and generous community sponsors.

Ping. Another message appeared on my phone.

After I read it, something happened. I felt different.

It was strange. I felt lighter inside.

"Mom! JB wants to know if I'd be an LIT next summer. Says to let them know ASAP. I need to take the training."

No answer. She'd already stepped out the door, phone to her ear, and hadn't heard me.

Using my crutches, I stumbled out to watch her open the car door. Our sidewalk was wet from the overnight storm. Overhead, through the broken clouds, the sun emerged behind the apartments across the street. In the distance, faint colours shimmered in the sky.

"Mom!"

She turned around, and walked back to where I stood. After I told her about JB's offer, she hugged me.

"Raven, you've been through some terrible things. And I wasn't always the best mom. But you're brave, and strong, and wonderful. You can do anything you want. I'm so proud of you." She hugged me again, then kissed my forehead.

The new feeling continued. It was hard to explain, but at the same time, I was thinking about JB. I felt an inner sensation, bright and colourful, changing me. Into someone different. A person without boundaries. It was a strange awareness, that didn't make a noise; instead, it had a *vibration*. One that I understood, deep inside.

It was the sound of hope.

I looked at the sky, squinted and held my breath. "Thanks, Mom. Will you do something for me, even if it seems silly?"

Then I pointed, and her eyes followed. A rainbow arched high above the distant condos and office towers.

"Do you hear that?" I said.

She blinked and opened her mouth, as if she wanted to say something. We stood in silence, and watched the bands of colour glitter and intensify, as the clouds drifted away.

"Sweetheart, I'm trying." Eyebrows furrowed, she tilted her head. "What do you hear?"

"The sound of a rainbow."

ACKNOWLEDGEMENTS

I wrote the entire first draft of *The Sound of a Rainbow* during a 72-hour marathon writing contest (minus a few hours of sleep). Thank you to organizers Karen Wehrstein, David Patterson, Krystyne Taylor-Smith, Jennifer Turney, Sharon Bacon, Shellie Westlake, Colum McNight and the hard-working team who put together the annual 72-hour Muskoka Novel Marathon competition in 2020. The event, held each July at the Canada Summit Centre in Huntsville, Ontario, is a fundraiser that supports the YMCA Simcoe-Muskoka Adult Literacy Program. I was fortunate to win the event in 2019 and 2020, and am grateful to the judges, my sponsors and cheerleaders. Thanks to Allister Thompson for his early editing suggestions.

I deeply appreciate the support of Heather Campbell of Latitude 46 Publishing, and her team, including Intern Emma Jay, who believed in this story. I owe a debt of gratitude, and appreciation to my editor Sarah Harvey for her thoughtful edits and coaching suggestions.

I'm grateful to fellow members of the Canadian Authors Association, Niagara, and the NOTL Writers' Circle for their insight during our critiquing sessions.

All the characters in this novel are fictional, but they were inspired by the many students I worked with during my educational career, and family members. Special thanks to my Halton District School Board mentors: Carolyn Neilson, Special Education Resource Teacher; Life Skills teacher Emily Moxey; the incredible Educational Assistants who worked with special needs students; Senior Administrators Ruth Peden, Mark Zonneveld; and Special Education Co-ordinator JoAnne Trigg.

I'm humbled to have had the opportunities to assist special needs students and their parents to find supportive equipment and placements, and to hire caring staff. Helping each child reach their unique potential is a privilege. I loved every minute of our joyful and exciting camping adventures! Even when the skunks came out at night.

I deeply value the benefits and healing powers of outdoor camp programs, and the opportunities for enrichment and empowerment that an immersive Arts education provides. My visits to the Aspen Valley Wildlife Sanctuary outside Rosseau, Ontario, and the work of its founder, Audrey Tournay were inspirational. Thank you to the talented staff members at summer camps across the country who deliver outstanding programs to exceptional needs children.

My wonderful husband, Bill French, my sons Matthew and Caley, daughter-in-law Danielle and granddaughters Camden and Lila are a source of ongoing love and support. Thanks to my mother, Alice Frayne; siblings, Linda, Sandra and Richard. And thanks to the memory of my father, Ralph H. Frayne who often said, 'Share, you've got a great imagination. You should write a book.'